He was real, all right. All too real.

All six feet and wide shoulders worth of him. He'd loosened his tie and his hair was all mussed and all she could do was stare, asking herself the same question her friend had. Why had she left such a man?

"Give me your keys. I'll change your tire."

Roused from her reverie, she remembered her disabled car. "I can do it. I don't need rescuing."

"Never crossed my mind. But even you can use a little help sometimes."

When he was done, Anne reached into the car and handed him disinfectant wipes.

Matt smirked. "A true nurse. Always prepared."

But when he stepped closer, she wasn't prepared. Not the least bit.

Why? They were over. She had moved on…to a safe life.

A lonely life, said an inner voice.

The more she was around Matt, the more confused she became. Or was she? Actually, what she wanted became clearer. But did she have the courage to reach for it?

Tina Radcliffe has been dreaming and scribbling for years. Originally from western New York, she left home for a tour of duty with the Army Security Agency stationed in Augsburg, Germany, and ended up in Tulsa, Oklahoma. Her past careers include certified oncology RN and library cataloger. She recently moved from Denver, Colorado, to the Phoenix, Arizona, area, where she writes heartwarming and fun inspirational romance.

Books by Tina Radcliffe

Love Inspired

The Rancher's Reunion
Oklahoma Reunion
Mending the Doctor's Heart
Stranded with the Rancher
Safe in the Fireman's Arms
Rocky Mountain Reunion

Rocky Mountain Reunion

Tina Radcliffe

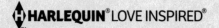
HARLEQUIN® LOVE INSPIRED®

 LOVE INSPIRED BOOKS

Recycling programs
for this product may
not exist in your area.

ISBN-13: 978-0-373-81886-0

Rocky Mountain Reunion

www.Harlequin.com

Printed in U.S.A.

Be of good courage and He shall strengthen your heart, all ye that hope in the Lord.
—*Psalms* 31:24

Acknowledgments

Many thanks to beta-reader Tracey Hagwood for her insightful comments and suggestions on the proposal for this book. Thank you, Maria King, RPh, for patiently answering questions related to diabetes. Thanks to Brenda at D and B House Movers in Monroe, Michigan, for being so helpful.

I'd like to add a shout-out to the Aarons in my life. Thank you, Tom Radcliffe, Tessie Russo, Michael Russo, Mary Connealy, Ruth Logan Herne, Missy Tippens, Debby Giusti, Janet Dean and Sharon Medley.

As always, thank you to my agent, Meredith Bernstein, for her support. A special thanks to my editor, Giselle Regus, who consistently challenges me to dig deeper and makes me a better writer.

Many of the Paradise series books are set in a fictional medical setting; however, the information in these works of fiction should never be considered a substitute for seeking medical advice. All errors are wholly mine.

Chapter One

"Anne, ambulances are en route."

Anne Matson looked up from the tidy pile of paperwork on her desk. "Was that *plural*?"

Marta Howard, RN, stood in the doorway of Anne's office. She reached up to tuck a strand of short gray hair behind her ear. "Afraid so. Accident at Paradise Lake. At the construction site."

Anne straightened the bud vase on her desk that held a fragrant pink rose bloom from her garden and put away her files.

"How far out are they?" She stood and grabbed her stethoscope before slipping a pen into the pocket of her navy scrubs.

"Seven minutes." Marta winked, her severe countenance warming. "And you thought it was going to be a slow day."

"I should have kept my mouth closed." Anne hit the light switch as she followed Marta into the emergency department hall. "What's the extent of the injuries?"

"The first is a male—thirty-two, in serious condition with broken ribs, upper quadrant and lower extremity lacerations, abrasions and possible internal injuries.

"Second patient is also a male, thirty-one, possible ankle fracture with minor abrasions and a head laceration. I've already paged Dr. Nelson. He's on his way."

"Surgeon on call?"

"Daniels."

"Notify him. Call Life Flight and give them a heads-up, in case we need transport."

"Got it."

As head of the Paradise ER nursing team, Anne was proud of her department, but she fully understood the limitations of the facility's trauma unit. The majority of the center's patients were the tourists that flooded the San de Cristo Mountain area and the close-knit mountain town of Paradise, Colorado, in search of seasonal recreation. Anything outside the scope of the small hospital's care would be transferred straight to Alamosa and often to Denver.

"What's going on with the patient in five?" Anne called out as Marta moved quickly to the unit secretary's reception desk.

"Discharged. I called Dr. Rogers."

"Sara?"

"No. Ben. He said he'd stop by tomorrow with his mobile unit and check the patient's incision."

Anne nodded and smiled. "That's why I like working in Paradise. All the efficiency of big-city medicine with the personal touch of rural medicine thrown in."

In the distance a siren could be heard. The familiar wail grew louder as the entire fleet of the Paradise Valley ambulance company approached the glass doors of the emergency department.

An instant later paramedics slammed through the ER doors. The late July heat met the hospital air-conditioning as a paramedic called out the first patient's stats while he steered the moving gurney.

Anne slid her hands into disposable gloves. "Get this one to triage," she directed. "The other can go to exam room two."

Marta and two orderlies followed alongside the gurney that sped into the curtained triage area while Anne grabbed the hospital copy of the paramedic's worksheet and shoved the papers into a metal chart.

"Move him over," Marta called. "On my count. One. Two. Three." The first patient was smoothly transferred to a hospital stretcher.

Anne noted the dwindling contents of the IV and hung a new bag as the medics left and Dr. Luke Nelson entered the room. Everything ran smoothly when Nelson was on the schedule.

Though he was new to Paradise, he was their most qualified ER physician.

"What do we have?" he asked, already assessing the patient.

"Scaffold accident." Anne read the chart. "Probable cracked ribs. Left abdominal-penetrating laceration, along with several minor lacerations to the scalp and face. BP is eighty-eight over fifty. Pulse, one hundred. Oxygen at three liters. Pulse ox, ninety percent."

He began a head-to-toe physical examination as an orderly sliced through the man's bloody shirt then wrapped an electronic blood pressure cuff around the patient's arm.

"Any relevant history?" Nelson asked as he peeled back the crimson-soaked abdominal dressing. He nodded to Marta and she applied a clean gauze pad.

"None noted," Anne said.

Nelson leaned over the patient. "Mr. Seville, I'm Dr. Nelson. We're going to take good care of you."

Seville? The name tripped a distant memory Anne couldn't quite grasp. Frowning, she dismissed the thought.

The dark-haired man, whose upper half of his face was obscured by dirt and blood and the lower part by an oxygen mask, gave a weak shake of his head.

"Open up that IV," Nelson continued. "I need

a CBC and chem panel. And type and cross for four units. Get X-ray down here stat."

"We've got another patient in exam room two," Anne said. She tossed her gloves and scrubbed her hands at a stainless-steel sink before leading the way down the hall.

"Are you going to the fund-raising dinner?" Luke Nelson asked, his steps in sync with hers.

"Apparently it's expected."

"You don't sound too enthusiastic."

"Don't I?"

He chuckled. "Politics, Anne. You have to play the game if you want to move up the career ladder. And since the money goes to expanding the emergency department, you should be excited."

Anne shook her head. Hospital social events were low on her list of things to be excited about. But Nelson was right. She'd have to try to be social for her career, because that was what she wanted, right? A career move; maybe even an administrative position.

Or maybe not. Lately she'd been restless for something that a promotion couldn't satisfy.

"Why don't we go together?" Luke finally asked.

She gave him a sidelong glance. "I have a rule about dating people I work with."

"Not a date." He shrugged. "Just going together."

"You're new to Paradise. Let me warn you

that the grapevine moves fast here. That's why I also make it a rule never to let the line between my job and my personal life blur. It's best to fly under the radar in this town."

"Sounds like you have a lot of rules."

Anne paused at his remark. Maybe she did. But the guidelines she'd set for herself had served her well as an unmarried woman living in a small town, and she didn't plan to detour anytime soon.

They reached the open exam room and she stopped short and handed the chart to him.

Luke flipped it open, scanned the contents and then handed the chart back to her as he moved into the small room. "Mr. Clark?" he asked.

"Matt. You can call me Matt."

"I'm Dr. Nelson and this is Ms. Matson."

Anne's head jerked back at the sound of Matthew Clark's voice and the chart in her hands tumbled to the floor. Her gaze snapped toward the clear blue eyes of the man she had married nearly eleven years ago.

"Anne?" His eyes widened in turn as he stared at her.

Matthew Clark sat on the edge of the exam table in a bloodstained, torn and once-white polo shirt and jeans. His shirt bore the logo of First Construction Company on the left chest area.

The ice pack he held to his head pushed back short, dark blond hair. His left foot was shoeless and encased in a temporary inflatable splint;

the right remained in a muddy steel-toed black work boot.

A bubble of air became trapped in Anne's throat and she had to remember to breathe.

Matthew.

The years had only improved his boyish good looks. He looked the same, from the dimple on the right side of his mouth to the tiny scar on his chin. The same, yet somehow different. Matthew Clark was a man now.

He grimaced. Clearly the swelling and already colorful contusions on his face were painful.

"You two know each other?" Luke looked back and forth between the patient and her, stunned interest on his face.

"She's my wife," Matt said, his voice flat and void of emotion.

Luke's brows shot up. *"Your wife?"*

"*Ex*. Ex-wife," Anne sputtered.

Her words stretched out, filling the small room with a million unanswered questions.

When Anne stooped to pick up the scattered chart at her feet her stethoscope slid to the tiled floor. Resisting a groan, she draped the stethoscope around her neck once more and gathered the papers. She read the paramedic's evaluation as she stood.

"How are you feeling?" Nelson asked his patient.

"I've been better," Matt returned. "I didn't think I needed that ambulance ride, but they insisted."

"Always good to play on the side of caution."

Anticipating the doctor's needs, Anne tore open a sterile package of gloves, and offered them to him. Maybe if she focused on her job, her thoughts would stop spinning out of control.

"Thanks." Nelson glanced at the hospital gown folded neatly and untouched next to Matt. "Ideally, we'd like you to change into that hospital gown."

"Me? In that? Not happening in this lifetime."

When a wicked smile curved his lips, Anne struggled not to laugh. Yes, the same old Matt. How had she forgotten his irreverent sense of humor?

The ER doc gave a thoughtful shake of his head. "We can work around it. I need to look at that scalp wound first."

Matt lowered the ice pack from his head.

"Not too bad. A couple of sutures should do the trick."

"You want to stitch my head?" He jerked back with surprise.

"Yes. These things bleed like crazy. Lots of superficial vessels in the scalp."

"Do you have to shave my head?"

"No. Just trim a bit of hair near the wound. Won't be obvious."

"Looks like I have to trust you."

"I'd appreciate that," Nelson said, matching his patient's humor.

"Go ahead and do what you have to do."

"I'll get a suture kit," Anne said.

She exited the room and leaned against the wall. Matt. After all these years? Releasing a deep breath, she grabbed a sterile suture kit from the supply cart. It tumbled from her trembling hands. Scooping it up, she turned and ran smack into Marta.

"Whoa, careful. Is Nelson in there?"

"Yes. Room two."

With a gentle hand on Anne's shoulder, Marta peered closely. "Honey, are you okay? You look pale. Maybe you're catching that bug that's going around."

"I'm fine."

"Hmm. Well, can you tell Nelson that the family of the patient in exam room three wants to talk to him?"

Anne nodded, avoiding her friend's gaze.

"You're sure you're all right," Marta persisted, her eyes probing with concern.

"I'm good." Of course she was good. As good as she could be after seeing the man she'd walked away from after they'd said, "I do."

Anne pushed back into the exam room. "You're wanted in three."

"On my way." Nelson turned to her. "Do you mind cleaning up that scalp wound? I'll be right back to suture and then we can send him up to X-ray to assess that ankle."

"No problem." Anne straightened her shoulders. Of course she could do this. She was a professional.

Nelson gave her a brief nod, pausing long enough to once again look from Matt to her as he exited.

"Could you go ahead and lie down, please?" she asked Matt.

"Lie down?"

Anne pulled supplies from the exam cupboards. "You're…" She cleared her throat. "You're too tall for me to reach the area."

The exam table creaked as he moved to a reclining position. "How's Manny?" Matt asked.

"Manny Seville." Anne turned slowly as realization hit. "Your college roommate."

"That's right. Manny is the site boss on the project."

"He's stable right now. We'll know more soon."

"Was his family notified? He has a wife and a new baby."

Anne released a small smile. "Does he? I always liked Manny, though I have to admit I never thought he'd settle down."

"People change."

Yes, they do.

She pulled herself from her musing thoughts. "Our procedure is to notify immediate family.

I can confirm that we had contact information when I finish this."

"Thank you," he said. Matt met her gaze, his expression humble. "I didn't mean to embarrass you in front of your—"

"Dr. Nelson is my colleague." She pulled the rolling stainless-steel exam table closer.

When he glanced pointedly at her left hand, her gaze in turn shifted immediately to his. Large, capable hands. In a heartbeat she regretted the action. There was no need to let him know that she'd often wondered if he'd married. After all, she'd moved on with her life long ago.

Hadn't she?

Matt glanced at her name tag: Matson RN. There was zero doubt in his mind that Anne hadn't told anyone about her "unfortunate" marriage.

Of course she had neatly erased the past. He expected nothing less.

Her black-brown hair framed her face in a bob that barely kissed her chin, the long bangs swept carelessly to the side, framing her face. Her features had evolved from a young, carefree girl to a classically elegant woman. He fought hard to ignore the fact that she was more beautiful now than at eighteen.

"So, you're a nurse," Matt said.

"Yes."

"Just like your aunt wanted."

Anne tensed a fraction, yet only silence ensued.

"Nine years," he finally murmured.

"Excuse me?"

"We haven't seen each other in nine years."

"Ten," she said, without looking up.

The simple response was enough to shake him to his core.

"Close your eyes, please. I'm going to cleanse the area and we don't want to get any Betadine in your eyes."

"Got it."

Her touch was gentle as she attended to his face. With his eyes closed he could smell the antiseptic along with a whiff of vanilla. Involuntarily, his lips curved into a smile. Anne always wore vanilla lotion. Why was it that solitary lingering memory stood out, pushing open the door to an onslaught of thoughts of what could have been?

He dared to peek at her once more, however her attention remained steadfast on her task. Then, as if sensing his perusal, her clear, dark eyes met his and held for a fraction, rounding in stunned surprise. She quickly glanced away.

"Aren't you going to ask what I'm doing in town?" Matt couldn't resist the question.

"Welcome to Paradise," Anne said with a rueful smile. "Everyone is already buzzing about the company that won the bid for the development down at Paradise Lake. I haven't seen this much excitement since the state put us on the map of Colorado."

She turned and smoothly grabbed a package from the table and tore it open. "How did this accident happen?"

"Pouring cement today. Long story short, the driver hit a piece of equipment. Manny and I were in the way."

"You're fortunate the injuries weren't worse."

"The Lord was watching out for us. That's for sure."

"So you're in construction instead of architecture?" she asked.

"Oh, I'm a residential architect. But it turns out I like being outside better than being trapped in an office."

"How long have you been with this company?"

"'This company' is mine." Pride underlined his words. "Mine and Manny's. We worked construction together overseas for a long time and finally decided we wanted to be our own boss."

"In Paradise? Why not Four Forks?" Her brows rose slightly.

"There's nothing for me in Four Forks. I haven't been back since I left for college. For the record, I'm in Paradise because we won the bid," he said, making it very clear that their past had nothing to do with his future.

The opportunity in Paradise had opened up just when he'd needed to put down roots for himself and his daughter. It would go a long way toward establishing his company in the Paradise Valley and providing them with the credibility to launch them into the big league. He felt God's hand on everything that had occurred in the past weeks…well, except for today's disaster.

"So you're not staying? This is temporary?"

"I'm not sure yet. We'll be headquartering somewhere in the valley." He bit back his irritation. "I can shoot you a memo when I decide, if that will help."

She frowned at his sarcasm, but said nothing, and Matt regretted his words. Somehow being around Anne for the first time in so many years brought out the bitterness he thought he'd moved beyond. Maybe forgiveness wasn't as easy as a simple prayer, after all.

When Matt began to shift on the gurney Anne put the weight of her forearm firmly against his shoulder, all the while maintaining the sterility of her gloved hands. Neat trick. She didn't look strong enough to hold a big guy like him pinned to the table. Yet she just did.

"Please don't move. I'm trying to remove some debris from the wound."

"Sorry." He closed his eyes against another wave of emotion brought on by the warmth of her arm against his shoulder.

Her touch still staggered him. That was worrisome. Very worrisome.

Silence stretched as she concentrated. "Got it," she finally said. The examination gloves snapped as she removed them. "All done. Now Dr. Nelson can suture the site."

"Great. Thanks." He grimaced as he sat up.

"What hurts?"

"What doesn't? Mostly my ankle."

"I'm guessing more than a little. It's likely that you have a fracture or at minimum a bad sprain. Once your lab work and X-ray are reviewed, I'll get the doctor to prescribe something for the pain."

"What I really need is to get out of here. I have to be somewhere." He reached to his back pocket and frowned. "Left my phone on the site."

"I can bring a phone into the exam room for you."

"Thank you. I'd really appreciate that."

"No problem. That's my job."

Right. Her job. *Nothing personal.* She'd effectively grounded him with those two words.

Then for the first time since she'd walked into the exam room, Anne really looked at him. Her deep brown eyes stared unflinching as though she was searching for answers. Then her cheeks pinked and she opened her mouth. No words came out. She winced as if in pain herself, finally glancing away.

She was remembering.

A small part of Anne Matson hadn't forgotten what they had once shared. The fleeting expression of remorse, sadness—or whatever had been on her face—unsettled him in a way that he hadn't felt in a very long time.

Matt swallowed and his breath caught in his chest. In truth, he'd planned for this moment for years; the moment he and Anne would come face-to-face again. He'd thought he was ready.

But he wasn't. He had to admit the truth. There was no way that he could have been prepared.

His racing thoughts froze. Why should her remembering the past give him pause?

Hours ago he would have vehemently denied the possibility that he needed confirmation that *they* mattered to her. Yet, there it was; an unspoken need deep inside him for Anne to at least acknowledge their history and the fact that she had walked away from what they'd had, shattering his life into ragged pieces.

He hadn't expected the victory to be quite so hollow.

All these years.

Once they were in love and now they were strangers. He'd torn their pages from his past and thrown them away long ago.

Yet here he was in Paradise, Colorado, with his memories and the reality of today slamming together.

He couldn't deny his confusion.

The wall of anger around his heart trembled and Matt swallowed, afraid. Until this moment he'd been certain that he was finally on the road the Lord had laid out for him. Finally, he had gotten his life together. Now he wasn't sure of anything.

Lord, I can't open myself up for that pain again. Protect me from myself.

Chapter Two

"He's your husband." Marta's words were a statement and not a question. Clearly her friend was shocked.

Anne's pen jerked, leaving a long line of ink on her paperwork. "Okay, who told you?" She quickly turned from the counter to glance around. The staff had thinned now that the crisis was over. Even the waiting room had emptied of patients waiting to be seen.

"Who do you think?"

"Luke Nelson."

"Of course." Marta shook her head. "The real question here is why am *I* the last to find out about this?"

Anne raised her hand into the air and help-lessly gestured. There was no good answer except that she'd never told anyone about what had happened ten years ago. How could she?

"I've known you since you graduated from

nursing school, Anne. Here I thought you were married to the job. So when did you have time to get married *and* divorced? And do not tell me you forgot. No one forgets a man who looks like that."

A giggling young nursing assistant moved past them, pushing Matt in a wheelchair, his left leg elevated. A wide grin lit up the young woman's face and infatuation sparked in her eyes.

"The nursing assistants did rock-paper-scissors to see who got to wheel him to X-ray."

"Oh, brother," Anne muttered, with a shake of her head.

"I heard the Paradise ladies auxiliary is already arguing over who gets to bring casseroles to his house."

"He's only been here an hour, how can they possibly work that fast? You're kidding, right?"

Marta lifted a brow. "Am I?"

Across from them laughter rang out as Juanita Villas, the plump, middle-aged unit clerk joined the conversation. "I signed up. Twice."

Anne's mouth dropped open.

"Don't look so shocked. *Me encanta*."

"And that means?" Anne asked.

"I like him. I like him a lot. He's quite charming," Juanita translated. "You've got good taste in ex-husbands."

"I'll say. Ruggedly handsome and tall. What is he, six-three? Four?" Marta mused, her gaze following to where the wheelchair was parked outside the elevator doors.

"Six-three."

Anne snapped her fingers in front of Marta when she didn't respond.

"Hmm?"

"Earth to Nurse Howard."

"Oh, sorry." Marta grinned. "I've apparently been married for way too long. All I can think is why would anyone ever divorce a man like that?"

"Annulment. Not divorce. I was eighteen years old. A baby for goodness' sake. And we were married for all of five hours before Aunt Lily put an end to my childish plan."

"F-five hours?" Juanita sputtered, her eyes round.

"That was what? Ten? Eleven years ago? I remember Lily back then."

"Back then?" Juanita commented.

"Oh, you're new to the valley. But I can tell you that Lily Gray was an important name around this area for years. A prominent real-estate developer and a very intimidating woman, as well," Marta said. "When Lily Gray said jump, people jumped."

"That was her public persona. She's always been a marshmallow to me," Anne said.

"Still, I can't imagine having her as your guardian," the older nurse continued. "It certainly explains a lot."

"What's that supposed to mean?"

Juanita and Marta exchanged knowing glances.

"Stop that, you two. Aunt Lil always did what she thought was best for me. I ran away to get married. She stopped me from making a huge mistake. How can I fault her for that?"

Marta shook her head. "Yet in all this time you've never mentioned your marriage. It must still be a sensitive subject."

"No. That's not it," Anne quickly denied. "I'm simply a private person. You know that."

Marta gave her a slow appraisal as she shook her head. "Hmm. I thought I knew you. But now I'm guessing maybe I don't. Never in a million years would I have pegged you for an impulsive act like running away to get married."

"Why not?"

Juanita snorted and wagged her index finger in the air. "Honey, I may only have arrived in town a few years ago, but even I know that Anne Matson doesn't do impulsive."

Though she searched for a response, Anne found none. Fine. Juanita was right. No matter how you looked at it, the facts were unchanged. She didn't do impulsive.

Indignation at the assessment had her narrowing her eyes at her coworkers and friends. "Look, I'd appreciate it if we could please keep this out of the Paradise grapevine."

"Of course," Marta said with her hand on her

heart and a nod to Juanita. "We know the rules. What happens in the ER…"

"Stays in the ER," Juanita said solemnly as she placed her hand over her own heart.

The desk phone rang and Juanita scooped up the receiver. She smoothly rolled her desk chair backward to grab an empty chart and pull a paper off the fax machine. "Yes, sir. We've got it." Hanging up the phone she looked to Anne. "Cardiac patient on his way. Wife is driving him in. Sudden onset of chest pain. That was his primary care doc from Denver. He instructed them to come in immediately. He's faxed over the history. Wife has a list of medications with her."

Marta peeked at Anne from over the top of her half-glasses. "We'll finish this conversation later."

Anne shook her head. Oh, no, they wouldn't. Not if she could help it.

The ER doors whooshed open and a middle-aged couple walked in. An orderly grabbed a wheelchair and assisted the patient into the seat as Juanita spoke to the wife.

"Exam room four," Anne called to the ER staff.

"CBC. Chem seven, cardiac enzymes, EKG and a chest X-ray. Get Cardiac down here to consult, please," Dr. Nelson directed as he moved toward the wheelchair.

"Anne."

Anne whirled around in time to see Sheriff Sam Lawson push through the glass doors. She looked back at the desk. "Marta, can you handle the cardiac patient? Sam's here."

Marta's gaze moved to the emergency room doorway. "Sure. Oh, by the way, the staffing agency called. Your aunt is threatening to fire another caregiver."

Anne groaned as she walked away. "Of course, she is." No day would be complete without her great-aunt being front and center on the agenda. "Tell them to ignore her threats. I do the hiring and firing."

Turning back to the sheriff, she smiled at her longtime friend and shook her head. Life would be a lot simpler if she could have fallen in love with someone safe like Sam. Instead her fickle heart had refused to be wooed by anyone since she and Matt had parted.

"Another fun day in Paradise?" Sam asked as he removed his tan Stetson.

"The usual."

"I find that Thursdays generally require extra prayer."

"Thursdays? Hmm, I had no idea. Why is that?"

"Everyone is in a rush to get to the weekend." He glanced around at the busy room. "How are thing here? I heard there was an accident at Paradise Lake."

"There was. We received both patients about

an hour ago and their status has been upgraded. One will most likely be discharged in a few hours and the other in twenty-four to forty-eight."

"And your aunt?"

"You heard Juanita?"

Sam nodded his head in affirmation.

"That's just Lily's usual 'off with their heads routine.'"

"Is her condition deteriorating?"

"Yes. She's more and more forgetful and she's taken to hiding things. Random things at that."

"Such as?"

"Yesterday I found the salt-and-pepper shakers under the couch cushions."

He chuckled. "That's not so bad."

"It depends on how much I need salt and pepper. The good news is that today she's in rare form and back to ruling the monarchy."

"I can stop by and check on her."

"Would you? She likes you. She seems somehow calmer when you're around."

He nodded toward the badge on his tan uniform shirt. "It's the badge. Seems to orient people." He grinned. "And no problem. Happy to do it."

"Thank you, so much. Key's under the mat if you should need it."

"Under the mat. Hmm. Well, since we're friends, I'll save my lecture on commonsense household security for another time."

"I appreciate that, too." Anne glanced out the door. "I thought you had something for me."

"I do. In my patrol car. Got a spare wheelchair?" he asked as he pulled a notebook from his starched uniform pocket.

"Are you transporting patients now?" Anne asked.

"This one was sleeping on a park bench outside the Paradise library. The librarian called me." He shrugged. "Since both ambulances were tied up and it's only three blocks, I brought her in."

Anne quirked a brow and looked past him to the parking lot. "What's the situation?"

"I'm not sure. Caucasian female. Around nine or ten years old. Can't put my finger on it, but she's lethargic and she smells funny."

"Drugs or alcohol?"

"She's a baby, and this is Paradise," Sam objected.

"Yes, and in a perfect world I wouldn't be asking you that. You're much too nice to be sheriff. You've got to get a little more cynical, like me."

"My deputy would argue that point with you. He says I need to lighten up."

She laughed. "Do you have a name for your admission?"

"No ID on her. She was with a black Lab whose collar says he's Stanley. They're both sleeping in my car. I'm taking the dog over to the vet's to board and check the tag registration."

"Why was a nine-year-old wandering around Paradise alone?" Anne mused. "I mean, where are her parents?"

"Must be tourists because I've never seen her or the dog before."

She shook her head and walked to the left of the admissions counter where a row of wheel-chairs was neatly parked. "Okay, let's get your Jane Doe in here."

An hour later and Anne was recalling Sam's advice about more prayer being needed on a Thursday.

She sat on a leather stool next to an emergency room bed while the girl Sam had brought in dozed. Anne flipped open the chart. Her stomach growled and she ignored the plea for sustenance, instead choosing to spend her lunch break with her youngest patient. The kid would be terrified if she woke up in a hospital all alone. Anne knew that feeling all too well.

The night she'd lost her both of her parents in a car accident remained etched in her mind forever. It was probably the reason she had chosen a career in medicine. The kindly nurse who had stayed with her in the hospital that night had made a huge impact on her. Now it was Anne's turn to return the favor.

A preliminary glucose check on the girl

showed elevated levels higher than the meter could read. Anne monitored the child's neuro status closely as they awaited lab results.

All indications were that the girl was well fed and cared for. Her jeans and shirt were clean, as was her long tawny-brown hair, parted neatly down the middle. So why was she sleeping on a public bench in the middle of the day? Alone. And who was she? What was her story?

The girl opened her eyes wide and immediately began fiddling with her hospital identification band and then with the IV tubing attached to her arm.

"Careful," Anne said gently. "We need that line. That's how we give you medicine."

The round honey-colored eyes stared through Anne as though she wasn't there.

"Can you tell me your name?" Anne asked.

"Claire" was the girl's thick reply. Her lids fluttered closed as though she had no more energy, her long lashes resting on pale skin accented by a sprinkling of light freckles. Rounded cheeks held the last evidence of childhood baby fat.

"Your last name?"

"Griffin."

"How old are you, Claire?"

"Nine." She blinked. "Where am I?"

"In the hospital."

Claire's eyes widened. "Am I going to die?"

"No. You're going to get better and go home. Can you tell me what happened today?"

The girl swallowed, as if her tongue was thick, but didn't answer.

Leaning forward, Anne offered her chilled water from a plastic cup with a straw. The girl eagerly drank and then leaned back again.

Anne lowered her face closer to the bed. "Claire, what happened today?" she repeated softly.

"I took Stanley for a walk and then I started feeling funny. So I sat down on the bench. I feel better now." She raised her head and glanced around. "Where's Stanley?" The whispered words were laced with panic.

"Stanley is fine. He's at the vet's. They're taking good care of him."

Claire's head sank back against the pillow.

"I need to contact your mother," Anne said.

One by one, a silent trail of tears rolled down Claire's cheek. She didn't wipe at them. It was as though she didn't even realize they were there.

Tightness pressed Anne's chest as she waited for the words she didn't want to hear.

"My mother is… She died," she said, her voice heavy and slow.

Oh, Lord. Not this little girl, too?

"I'm so sorry," Anne murmured, knowing the words were ineffectual at best. Before her brain registered what she was doing, she reached out to hold Claire's free hand and give it a squeeze. "My momma died when I was your age."

"Maybe they're in heaven together," Claire whispered.

Anne nodded, surprised yet pleased at the words.

The girl was silent, as though considering the possibility.

"Where's your father, Claire?"

"Call Delia. I stay with Delia during the day. She lives on Maple Street by the church."

A knock on the door to the exam room preceded Marta's entrance. Anne stood and joined Marta in the hall, leaving the door ajar so she could watch Claire.

"Labs?" Anne asked.

Marta nodded. "Tox screen came back negative. Blood alcohol negative. Glucose six hundred."

Anne shook her head. "Thanks, Marta. Tell Nelson we need insulin dosing ASAP."

"Done. He's on the way."

"You're good," Anne commented.

"I sit at the feet of the master." Marta quietly chuckled as Anne slipped back into the room.

"Claire, has anyone ever told you that you're diabetic?"

"I don't know what that is."

"You haven't been to the doctor recently?"

"No. There's nothing wrong with me. I never get sick."

"Phone for you, Anne," Juanita called from the open doorway.

Anne stood.

"No. Don't go." Claire voice was laced with panic and she reached out a hand to stop Anne, her fingers clinging to the scrub shirttail.

Juanita lifted her brows.

"I'll be right back. I promise." Anne held the girl's hand for a moment and smiled.

"She likes you," Juanita said, confusion in her eyes as she glanced from the bed to Anne.

"Thanks for the vote of confidence there, pal," Anne returned.

"The kids usually bond with Marta. She's the mothering type. That's all I'm saying."

Anne's head swiveled to Juanita. "Excuse me?"

"Sorry, boss. I just meant…"

"This one has been through a rough time. I can relate. She reminds me of myself at her age."

"Now you're going to try to tell me that you were a kid once?" Juanita asked with a teasing grin.

"You're a real hoot today, aren't you?"

"Every day. All part of my job description."

Anne washed her hands and followed Juanita down the hall. "Can you call up to Pediatrics for a bed? Nelson will no doubt admit her until her glucose levels are stable. Her name is Claire Griffin."

"Will do. Any luck contacting a responsible party?" Juanita asked when they stopped at reception. She nodded her head toward her computer. "Insurance information would be real nice."

"All I have so far is the name." Anne grabbed the blinking phone on the counter. "Matson, here."

"Anne, it's Sam. I just had a call from a Delia Seville. She's hysterical. Says her husband is in the ER. She doesn't have any transportation to hospital, and on top of that, her friend's little girl is missing. Apparently, Mrs. Seville was babysitting."

"Seville? One of the two men from the construction accident is Manny Seville. We admitted him."

"Was the other guy Matthew Clark? First Construction?"

"Yes. He's still here. Right now he's in Orthopedics being evaluated. Why?"

"I think that's his little girl I brought in. The Seville woman says she was with a black Lab."

Anne nearly gasped aloud.

Matt has a daughter?

"Anne? You still there?"

"Yes. Sorry. Sam. The girl's name is Claire Griffin."

"That's her."

"I'll have someone notify Matthew Clark."

"Thanks. I'm going to give Mrs. Seville and her baby a ride to the hospital."

"Her husband's stable. Tell her that. And thanks, Sam." Anne put down the phone.

Matt has a daughter? Her mind played the words over and over. Well, what did she expect? That his life was going to stop when she walked out on him?

She turned to Juanita. "I've got a responsible party to sign your insurance paperwork on that little girl."

"Thank you." Juanita's eyes lit up.

"Matthew Clark. He's still upstairs. Tell him we have his daughter down here and get him to sign the permission to treat while you're at it."

Juanita shook her head. "Aw, now you're going to ruin my day. Do not tell me that man has another wife."

"Another wife?"

"Besides you, I mean."

Anne could feel her facing warming. "I don't know anything about Mr. Clark, Juanita, but I feel confident you're going to find out."

"You know me too well." She scooped her clipboard off the desk and headed toward the elevators.

Anne gripped the counter and turned to stare at the wall. She did the math. *A nine-year-old daughter.*

That would be shortly after her aunt had had the marriage annulled and transferred her from the University of Denver to Washington State to finish her degree.

She'd spent the better part of three years completely heartbroken but unwilling to defy her aunt. Her sole guardian.

Aunt Lily had warned her that a future with Matthew Clark was building her house on unstable ground. He was a penniless student with no prospects. Love, she'd claimed, was fleeting, especially when there was no money in the bank.

All these years, and her aunt had been proved correct. Anne had mistaken what she and Matt had had for love. Clearly he had no such illusions and had moved on with his life quickly enough, as though their love had never existed.

Matt stood in the door of his daughter's room, resting his weight on his new aluminum crutches.

"Mr. Clark, you're just in time," the nurse who stood at Claire's bed said. "I'm Megan Jansen, the diabetic nurse educator."

He bit back a surge of pain as he moved into the room and shook her hand.

"Are you okay?" she asked with a quick glance down at his ankle in the plastic support boot.

He nodded. Yeah, he was okay. Glad to have dodged the need for surgery, but a badly sprained ankle requiring a walking boot and crutches wasn't what he had expected when he'd rolled out of bed this morning.

"We were about to go over the use of the meter," Megan said with a soothing tone. "I've got a warm washcloth to clean Claire's hand and stimulate the flow of blood to her finger."

"I don't want to," Claire responded. She forcibly tugged her hand away and turned her head toward the window.

"We can't discharge you until you or your father demonstrates the ability to use the meter and administer the injections."

"*He* can do it," Claire said. The words were a sullen accusation, as though Matt had added yet another heap of misery into her young life.

Matt feared she was right.

Across the room, Megan Jansen's gaze pleaded with Matt to intervene.

"Claire, we want you to get better," Matt said.

"There's nothing wrong with me. I feel fine."

The nurse stood and moved her equipment to the bedside table. "I think it's time for your father to try. The sooner we get this done and get you home, the better."

"He's not my father and I don't have a home..." Claire's voice trailed off and her eyes filled with moisture.

Matt's gut clenched. Could he blame her? Claire's world had been turned upside down in the past month. She'd gone from living with her mother in Denver one day to living with a man she didn't know the next.

Confusion registered on the nurse's face as she looked at him. "I thought you were her father."

"I am—"

"I want Anne," Claire interrupted with a pitiful wail.

"Anne?" Megan asked, her gaze moving from Claire to him, her brow furrowed yet again.

"Claire, who is Anne?" Matt asked, as a prickle of apprehension swept over him. Surely she didn't mean...

"That nurse," his daughter answered.

"From the emergency room?" he asked.

"The ER nursing supervisor," Megan clarified.

"She's the supervisor?" he countered.

"Yes." She glanced at her watch and nodded toward the door, indicating he should follow.

Matt hobbled outside the room right behind her.

"Why is she asking for Anne?" Megan asked.

"I have no idea. Claire was admitted while I was in X-ray."

"You know she's off duty now, right?"

Matt could only nod and raise a palm. What was he supposed to do now?

"My mother is a very close friend of Anne's. I can call her. She'll try to get in touch with—"

"No. I can't...I can't bother her." Especially not after his lousy attitude in the exam room.

"I think you'd better." Megan paused. "What other choice do you have?"

"Why tonight? Can't we wait until morning? After the doctor checks on her? Claire's spending the night anyhow."

"Anne might not even be scheduled to work tomorrow. I think it would be prudent for me to at least have my mother call her."

"But you said I could do the injections and testing."

"Look, Mr. Clark, unless you plan to be with Claire twenty-four-seven, she needs to participate in her own care. Sure, I can okay her discharge, but that won't help you or Claire in the long run. Your daughter has provided us with an option, and if Anne's presence will engage her, well, then…" She raised her shoulders and stared pointedly at him. "You should be willing to try this route."

He glanced from the nurse through the doorway to his daughter. Claire's eyes were closed in an attempt to block out the world. He felt like doing the same thing right about now.

Instead he fought back his pride and battled against the humiliation of the thought of inviting Anne Matson into his spectacular failure of a life as a new father.

Matt took a deep breath. "Okay. If it will help Claire. Yeah. Go ahead and ask your mother to get in touch with Anne."

Megan left and he moved back into the room to stand at the window and stare out at the Paradise skyline. Clear blue skies, dotted with clouds, stretched as far as he could see. In the distance, mountain peaks hovered at the edge, guarding the small mountain community.

As a child he had looked out windows at the very same view. Always asking the same questions he was asking now. *Where are you in all this, Lord?* He silently prayed. *Are you listening?*

How had he come full circle back to the one place on the planet where he felt so vulnerable? Paradise Valley.

He ran a hand over his face and shook his head. Seemed everything had gone from good to messed up; his business, his friend Manny and even Claire. Now he was about to be challenged further. He was about to welcome the woman who'd once destroyed him back into his life. The woman was virtually a stranger to his daughter, yet Claire had chosen Anne over him to support her during this crisis. How was that for irony?

Chapter Three

Anne pulled into her driveway and sat in her pickup, staring at the house and mustering the energy to climb the steps while desperately grasping for a peace she didn't feel.

Normally she could count on separating her two worlds by the time she had driven home. The sight of the two-story Victorian home signaled the boundary line as she put the day job behind her. The house calmed her, no matter the crisis in the Paradise ER.

But for the first time in her life *calm* was out of the question. Seeing Matt Clark and meeting his daughter had knocked her world into chaos and she didn't like it one bit. Her life had an orderly precision and she blamed the past intruding on her present for today being completely out of control.

She began to pray under her breath while staring at the lovely building in front of her. It had wide steps that led to a cherry-red door topped with a stained-glass transom. The siding was painted dark cream with sea-foam-green accents. Scalloped cedar trimmed the second story, always reminding Anne of a gingerbread house. On the left was a small turret room that rose above the second floor.

This year she'd had the entire house repainted. Next summer's goal was refurbishing the back deck. With a house that was over one hundred years old, there was always something that needed repair.

This particular home was the only connection she had left to family. And that family was only her great-aunt Lily.

Lately Anne never knew what to expect when she arrived home. Sometimes it was the dynamic and formidable Aunt Lily of Anne's childhood, other days her aging great-aunt was disoriented, showing more and more indications of the insidious Alzheimer's disease. Their roles had somehow become reversed. Now Anne found herself the caregiver for the woman who'd taken her in as an orphan some twenty years ago.

She gripped the steering wheel tightly, fighting back the questioning resentment that simmered just below the surface as her mind continued to race with thoughts and mental images of Matt and Claire.

For the first time since all those years ago she began to question the choices that were made for her when she was eighteen.

Ten years ago Lily had told her that education, a career and the independence to make her own choices was the important thing. Deep down inside she feared her aunt had been wrong. Those may have been the right choices for Lily Gray, but had they been the right choices for Anne Matson?

And if not, wasn't it too late to do anything about it anyhow?

When the front door swung open and her aunt stepped outside and waved, urging her out of the truck, Anne did a double-take. She quickly reached for her leather tote and climbed out of the vehicle.

"Aunt Lily, is everything okay? Where's your walker?"

"Oh, I don't need that thing." Petite and trim, her aunt gripped the rail tightly and held herself up with dignity. She always wore a dress, no matter the day or hour, looking for all the world like the queen of the manor.

"Okay," Anne answered slowly. She glanced past her aunt to the open doorway. "And you aren't wearing your alert necklace."

"That's for people who might fall. I'm fine."

"And your aide?"

Lily shared a satisfied grin and ran a hand through her silver curls. "I sent her home. For good."

There was a challenge in her aunt's words and Anne wasn't going to feed into it.

Yet, despite herself, a groan of frustration slipped from her lips. Sometimes her aunt Lily bamboozled her caregivers into thinking she didn't need help and sent them home. Other times she simply fired them on the spot. Once again Anne would need to call the staffing agency.

She walked up the drive to the porch, her steps weary. "Why did you fire your aide?"

"That woman makes me have uncharitable thoughts. I can tell you that the good Lord would not be happy with that."

"Aunt Lily. You know her replacement will be here tomorrow." She moved up the cement steps and placed a kiss on her aunt's forehead.

Lily offered a satisfied smile. "Oh no, dear. Not tomorrow. They can't get another one until Monday at the earliest. I already called for you."

"You called?"

Lily nodded.

"Tomorrow is Friday. I have to work. I can't stay home."

"You work too much. You and I could play hooky tomorrow." Lily wiggled her brows suggestively.

Anne ushered her aunt into the house ahead of her. "I can't do that."

"Of course you can. You never call in sick. You never take a day off. Why, I imagine you have enough vacation time accumulated to take a trip around the world."

Lily suddenly swayed and Anne reached out to grab her arm. "Where's your walker?"

"Oh, phooey."

"Aunt Lily?"

"It's in the hall closet."

Anne pulled open the closet door and slid out the walker, placing it squarely in front of her aunt.

"You know I'm still your elder," Lily stated.

"I know that, Aunt Lily. I also know that I love you and I don't want you to get hurt. Please use your walker."

Lily released a huff of disgust.

When the house phone rang, Anne reached around her aunt to grab the receiver, grateful for the reprieve.

"Anne. Oh, good. I tried your cell and you didn't answer."

"Marta. Sorry. When I get outside Paradise town limits there are pockets where I get absolutely no signal. What's up?"

"Megan called me."

"Your daughter? Is everything okay?"

"Yes. She was assigned as diabetic nurse instructor for your patient."

"What patient?"

"That little girl. Claire."

"Oh?" Anne moved to the dining room and dropped her bag on the floor. "Is she okay? Is her father still there?

"Oh, yes, Mr. Hunky has been at her bedside since you left. She's stable but she refuses to learn how to use the monitor or anything. Megan asked me to call you."

"I don't understand. Why would Claire ask for me?"

"You made some kind of impression on the kid. Frankly, Meg is a little concerned about the home environment. Apparently the girl lost her mother and really doesn't know her father. Social Services is asking us to assist on this one. After all, she was found on a park bench. Maybe you could check things out."

"I'm confused. How does Meg expect me to evaluate the situation?"

"Diabetic instruction. Didn't I say that?"

"No, you didn't."

"Sorry. Let me start over." Marta gave a slightly embarrassed chuckle. "The endocrinologist has agreed to discharge tomorrow afternoon if Claire's blood glucose levels continue to improve, but only if you agree to assist with diabetic instruction."

"*What*? Marta! Me? I'm not even sure I'll be in tomorrow." Anne pushed back her bangs. "We've got some caregiver issues here with my aunt again."

"Well…" Marta hesitated. "They could go to your house."

"That's crazy. They can't come here."

"Company?" Her aunt chirped from behind her. "I'd love to have company. The rose garden is so beautiful this time of year. We could have a picnic. Tell them yes, Anne."

"Aunt Lily, isn't it time for your game show?" Anne inched farther into the dining room.

"So it's a little unconventional," Marta continued. "But this is Paradise. We don't do things the same way they do in the big city. You said so yourself, remember?"

"Of course, I did. I'm always saying things that will come back to haunt me." Anne was silent, her gaze following her aunt, who had settled into a favorite recliner.

"This isn't about Matthew Clark, is it?" Marta said quietly. "Because if it is, I think you should put your feelings for him aside."

Feelings? Did she have feelings for the man? She'd barely touched the surface of sorting through her emotions after running into Matt. The entire day had been simply exhausting; that was the only feeling she was sure of.

"Are you still there?"

"I'm here, Marta."

"What happened between you two is in the past, isn't it?"

Anne sighed. The past. A wonderful place where she'd like to hide right now.

Instead she turned away from the living room and whispered into the phone. "Absolutely, and I couldn't agree more. I was very young and, yes, that was a long time ago."

"Then it shouldn't be a problem, right?"

Anne became silent. Should it be a problem? No. She could be a professional and handle the situation. But would her aunt remember Matt after all these years? And if she did, would she say something inappropriate, embarrassing or humiliating for both Anne and Matt?

That scenario seemed highly unlikely with Lily's current state of mental health. In all probability she wouldn't remember Matt at all. Still, everything inside Anne screamed that this was a bad idea. At very least it would be awkward. Anne couldn't help but be nervous about the possibilities for disaster.

"Are you there?" Marta asked.

"Yes." She paused again. "I'm thinking."

"Think about this. Claire Griffin is a motherless little girl with an emotional hole in her heart. She's reaching out to you."

"Oh, that's not fair," Anne murmured through the lump in her throat.

"Perhaps. But it's the absolute truth."

"Marta, I just don't…" She took a deep breath. "The situation is all kinds of impossible."

"Forgive me if I'm out of line here, Anne, but if Claire's father can humble himself to ask you for help, then I think you should consider doing the same."

"I hate it when you're right."

"That's what friends are for."

Anne sighed loudly. "Okay. Fine. Take me off the schedule for tomorrow and give Matt Clark a call."

"Thank you."

"I should pray that I don't regret this," Anne muttered into the receiver. "But I already do."

"Claire, we leave in ten minutes," Matt called upstairs.

As usual, there wasn't a single sound in response to his announcement. The two of them lived in the little cottage, yet all he ever heard was the echo of his own voice and Stanley's occasional barking.

Matt glanced at the clock. After Claire's discharge, he had agreed to let her come home to shower and change clothes before they headed to Anne's. That might have been a tactical error since he knew very little about how long it took young girls to shower and dress.

He pulled his phone from his back pocket and

typed a few more items onto his already-lengthy virtual grocery list. When he pulled open the door of the fridge and rested against the appliance, he could only shake his head. A lonely foil-covered casserole greeted him.

The nurse educator had laid out Claire's nutritional needs. Apparently the haphazard meal plans he'd been providing up to now weren't exactly going to win him any awards for father of the year. It's wasn't as though he'd had a childhood of healthy eating habits to draw upon.

Nope. His only parent was an alcoholic and they usually didn't worry much about the food pyramid. So here he was learning how to read nutrition labels and practice smart meal choices not only for his daughter but to set a good example, for himself.

Thankfully some of the women in town had felt sorry for him and brought by lasagna and a fresh tossed salad last night. The meal was the first home-cooked fare since his last invitation to Delia and Manny's house. And the good news was that there were leftovers.

He hobbled across the room, careful not to bear weight on his injured ankle, and nearly stumbled into the table in the process. Disgusted with himself, he sank into the chair. It hurt, but he couldn't rely on pain pills if he was going to drive.

Hopefully he'd be able to get things back on

track by the end of the day. How things had gotten so off course in a mere twenty-four hours he wasn't sure. God had led him to Paradise but at some point Matt had stopped listening.

There was no doubt his pride was his undoing. He had to admit that since the moment he'd landed the job in Paradise, he had hoped to run into Anne so he'd be able to show her and her aunt what a success he'd made of his life. In the scenario that ran through his mind, she'd walk away from their meeting bemoaning the fact that she'd left him.

Things hadn't turned out the way he'd expected. Not by a long shot. Yes, he'd been prideful and disaster had ensued. Now he found himself humbled and reaching out to Anne, of all people, for help.

Why was it that it took him so long to realize that every single time he took a step out without God's direction he fell flat on his face?

Matt felt Stanley's concerned and baleful eyes locked on him. The dog nudged him with his nose.

"Good boy," Matt crooned as he rubbed the animal's head. The Lab's tail began to rhythmically thump on the tiled floor. Matt dipped his hand into the biscuit jar on the table and offered one to the pooch.

Thank you, Lord, for Stanley. The dog had stuck by Claire when she'd gotten sick yesterday.

Things could have been a lot worse if Stanley hadn't been around.

So far the best thing he'd done since gaining custody of Claire was to bring Stanley into their lives. The rescue dog had been his idea, to give the little girl something to focus on besides her loss.

The plan had worked and in return the Lab had never left her side. He had taken better care of Claire than her own father. What did that say about his parenting skills? He hadn't even picked up on the signs that something was wrong with his child.

Tonight was going to be another test. He had to wake her in the night to test her glucose levels with the meter. Could he handle that? What if he slept through the alarm? What if he forgot everything the nurse had taught him?

Claire's life depended on him.

Diabetes. The diagnosis terrified him and he fought not to let her know how scared he was. She might go into diabetic ketoacidosis if her blood sugar got too high or, worse, if he had to actually use the glucagon kit the hospital had given them for low blood sugar.

He'd been through a lot of things in his life, but he'd only had himself to worry about. Now he was responsible for two people and it was a first for him.

Matt ran a hand through his hair and stared

ahead, seeing his daughter's face as she'd slept in the hospital bed. Her long hair spread on the pillow, she'd looked more like six years old than nearly ten.

Suddenly everything in his life shifted. The seriousness of Claire's disease left him reeling. Nothing was more important than his daughter.

His daughter.

She'd lost her mother and now had to rely on a father she didn't know. It hadn't helped any that he had been out of the country for most of the past ten years. When he'd finally met Claire they were like strangers. The irony was that they were the only family they each had left.

Emotion choked him and he pushed aside the stack of diabetic literature on the table, fighting anger. Rage aimed at himself mostly, because there was no point in harboring a grudge against the woman who had kept his child a secret. He was as guilty as she was for their reckless act of impulsiveness. Claire was the one caught in the middle. She'd never known her father and now her mother was gone.

In the center of the table sat his Bible. He hadn't touched it since church last Sunday. Matt pulled the soft, leather-covered book closer. When he flipped through the pages the bookmark tucked in the very middle stopped him. Of course he knew what he would find nestled next to Psalm 31: a photo of him and Anne on their wedding day. Some days the picture made him smile. Other days the pain remained unbearable.

Today he closed the book as quickly as he'd opened it.

He glanced at his watch again. "Five minutes, Claire."

Stanley barked as Claire entered the kitchen a moment later.

Her face was unreadable and expressionless as usual. Damp brown hair fell in waves past her shoulders. She wore a pink hoodie and blue jeans. He could have dealt with anger and defiance. That had been his attitude du jour, growing up with an absentee mother and a drunken father. But this indifference? Matt had no idea how to reach through the wall she'd constructed. He was an adult and he was afraid of a nine-year-old.

"Where are we going?" she asked, her face a mask.

"To see your new friend, Anne."

A tiny light flickered in her brown eyes. "The nurse?"

"Yes. I called and we're going to her house for some diabetic instruction."

Claire's shoulders relaxed imperceptibly. "Thank you," she breathed.

Matt nodded, realizing that he had done something right. That surprised him, though he wasn't going to pat himself on the back just yet. One step at a time. That was his new motto.

Claire was pleased and that was a good thing.

"How about if you grab the testing supplies and then get Stanley into the truck for me?"

She nodded.

When they were settled, he punched Anne's address into the GPS and they drove in silence toward the outskirts of Paradise, past Patti Jo's Café and Bakery, the hardware store and several novelty shops. Pedestrian traffic was steady in the small town where giant planters of geraniums and trailing ivy decorated the sidewalks.

Summer brought tourists escaping the heat of Denver and Colorado Springs to the moderate-to-cool climate of the mountain town for fishing, hiking and other activities. The town was picturesque and quaint, nestled in the San Luis Valley with the Sangre de Cristo Mountains to the north and the San Juan Mountains to the west.

As they started outside of town onto a rural road something began to click in Matt's mental map. Anne lived on the other side of the lake. They'd met in college and he'd never actually been to her house, though he'd lived just a couple of miles northwest in the even smaller town of Four Forks. She'd never wanted him to meet her great-aunt, as though she'd suspected all along that her guardian would disapprove of their relationship.

That should have been his first red flag. But he'd been young and had thought that love conquered all—including his "wrong side of the tracks" background. Now he knew to listen to those warning flags as a spiritual first line of defense. Today the closer they got to Anne's house the more his radar alarmed loud and clear.

He drove for a few miles following the directions on the GPS map, all the while watching for a location where he could safely pull off and onto the shoulder. Easing the truck to the right, he put on his emergency flashers.

"What are you doing?" Claire asked.

"Just checking something." Matt reached into the backseat and pulled out the project plans. He carefully removed the sheath from the cardboard cylinder and unrolled the inner documents.

"Can you hold this?"

Claire held one side of the huge blueprint and he held the other.

His heart hammered. Sure enough. The very plans he'd helped create were about to complicate his life. Big-time.

Plans on paper were supposed to be adjustable. Erase them, start over and redo the mistakes. Right?

Well, it was too late for that. Everything had been set in motion. Official documents had been approved and registered. Construction had begun. Demolition permits had been filed.

The map that lay on the plans spread in front of him indicated that straight ahead they would turn right onto a narrow road. The town, in consultation with his firm, planned to expand and widen this particular rural road, providing a very necessary secondary egress to Paradise Lake and the development homes and condos.

Urban renewal—except this time it was in the country. But the theory was the same. The town of Paradise had the right of eminent domain: a legal instrument to move people and property for development projects that improved the town.

In Paradise that meant that all three of the houses along that road were slated to be razed. Homeowners had been given generous market value offers and they'd receive positive responses from all but one.

The single holdout, by virtue of no response, was address twenty-two-fifty.

Too late, he realized that twenty-two-fifty was the house that belonged to Lily Gray.

What were the odds?

Ten years later and Anne still lived with her aunt. Matt fought the desperate urge to turn the truck around, go back home, pack his bags and head straight to Denver.

If that wasn't bad enough, and it absolutely was, he realized he was about to come face-to-face with Lily Gray after all these years. The woman he blamed for turning Anne against him. For destroying the happy ending he'd planned for his life.

He began to roll up the blueprint, carefully tucking the document back into the protective tube.

"Is something wrong?" Claire whispered in her soft voice.

Matt released a breath and rubbed his jaw. "Yeah. You could say that."

"What is it?"

"Hard to explain," he answered. "But it's nothing that a little prayer won't fix."

Claire frowned slightly and cocked her head, her amber eyes clear. "Do you pray about everything?"

"I try to." He turned and fully faced his daughter. "Do you pray, Claire?"

"I guess." She shrugged. "Sometimes."

"That's good, because God is the best daddy either of us has. He won't ever let us down. Today I am definitely going to need His help. And if today is one of those 'sometimes' for you, I'd like a few prayers, as well."

She blinked and studied him, as though digesting his words, and then offered him a small nod.

The gesture comforted him as he signaled and got back on the road.

After driving a quarter mile farther he turned right. He saw the house long before the GPS device announced their arrival. This was the house Anne had talked about all the time when they were together. The home she was raised in as an orphan by her aunt. He'd recognize the cookie-cutter-trimmed Victorian from her descriptions. Architecturally he could appreciate the amazing structure with its period corbels, fish-scale shingles and cedar shakes.

Matt regretted that he hadn't actually looked at the house before this, instead relying only on the geographic maps to plan the construction.

Would he have changed his mind and found another way to the lake if he'd seen how unique it was? If he'd known it was Anne's home?

He'd never know for sure. "That's her house?" Claire breathed.

"Looks like it is."

"It sort of looks like a castle," she said, talkative for the first time ever.

"What makes you think that?"

"Look at that pointy room there with the long windows."

"A turret."

"Turret," she repeated. "That's a room where a princess lives. Like Rapunzel."

"A princess," Matt murmured. He shook his head, trying to see the big house from his daughter's eyes.

"I never thought about it that way, Claire. But I can see you're absolutely right."

Yeah, it was a castle with a princess inside. A

dark-haired princess with chocolate-brown eyes who apparently had no clue that her castle was under siege.

Chapter Four

"They're here," Aunt Lily called. Excitement bubbled over in her voice. "Oh, hurry, hurry."

"I'm right behind you." Anne smoothed her hair and took a deep breath as her aunt pulled back the heavy, paneled curtains for another peek.

"My, isn't he handsome?" Lily said, cocking her head to the side. "He looks a little familiar. Do I know him?"

Anne swallowed and began a hasty prayer under her breath.

"Oh, look they brought their dog," she announced.

"He's a big fellow."

"Yes. Six foot three."

Lily laughed. "I meant the dog." She turned to Anne and smiled. "My, you look lovely, dear."

"Thank you." Anne glanced down at her black slacks and rose-print blouse and removed a small thread. She tucked her hair behind her ear and fussed with her bangs.

She'd obsessed over what to wear this morning, finally deciding to go casual yet professional. However, confidence in her apparel and being fully prepared to instruct on Type 1 Diabetes still failed to take the edge off her churning stomach or to still her trembling hands.

When the doorbell rang Aunt Lily carefully maneuvered her walker down the short hall. She straightened her dress and pushed her shoulders back, ready to greet her guests. A huge grin lit up her elfin face as Anne opened the door.

"Hello, hello," Lily brightly called.

Behind the screen stood Matt, bigger than life on crutches, with Claire by his side, her arms protectively crossed. A pink backpack with all her diabetic supplies hung from her wrist. Stanley panted eagerly, ready for action, though he obediently waited on the sidewalk, his tail slapping the cement.

"Ma'am." Matt nodded and met Anne's gaze. His was apologetic and revealed the depth of his nervousness. "I'm sorry for the inconvenience."

"It's not a problem." She smiled at his daughter. "How are you feeling, Claire?"

"Better," the little girl murmured.

"Aunt Lily, this is Mr. Clark and his daughter, Claire."

"How wonderful to meet you," Aunt Lily said

with enough perky energy and enthusiasm to cover the potential awkwardness of the moment.

Confusion registered on Matt's face as he stared at Lily. He quickly regrouped.

"Pleased to meet you, Ms. Gray."

"Call me Lily. Oh, we're going to be friends. I can see that." She glanced at his ankle boot and crutches. "What happened?"

"A little accident."

"Oh, I'm so sorry."

Still looking perplexed, Matt held up a dog dish and a water bottle. "Would it be okay for Stanley to wait out here?"

"We can do better than that," Lily said. "The backyard has a little gazebo. He could wait there and have some shade."

"Thank you, ma'am."

"I like your house," Claire said, her gaze moving past Anne and Lily to peek down the long front hall.

"Well, thank you, dear. It is very special."

"Claire says it reminds her of a castle," Matt added.

"A castle?" Lily smiled at the girl. "You're very right. That's exactly what my grandmother had in mind when the house was built for her."

Lily turned to Anne. "Why don't you show Mr. Clark and his dog the way to the backyard?

This young lady and I will meet you there. I'll give her a little tour of our home along the way."

Claire's eyes widened with delight and Anne could only blink with pleasant surprise at her aunt's take-charge attitude as she held open the door and ushered Claire in. Today Aunt Lily was very lucid and Anne couldn't help but wonder if it was Claire who was responsible.

"Your aunt isn't exactly what I remembered," Matt said as he tucked his crutches beneath his arms.

"Ten years is a long time. And as I recall, you had about twenty minutes in her presence."

"Yeah, well, *as I recall*, twenty minutes was pretty much all I needed."

Anne could hardly refute his words. Her aunt had been ruthless in her dismissal of Matt, forbidding Anne from contacting him in any way, shape or form.

The two of them were silent as Stanley led the way, trotting gingerly on the wide, shale paver path along the side of the house and pausing on occasion to wait for Matt to catch up on his crutches.

Were they both thinking of the past?

"Your aunt really doesn't remember me?"

"Not today she doesn't. She has some vascular dementia and was recently diagnosed with Alzheimer's. Some days her personality, temperament and memory fluctuate like the weather."

He frowned. "Claire will be okay with her?"

Anne stiffened. "Yes. Of course. She's not dangerous."

"Sorry. I'm not familiar...I didn't mean to imply..." He shrugged.

She knew she should say something gracious to let him off the hook, but the words eluded her. The situation was becoming more awkward by the minute, just as she'd feared.

When they passed the corner of the house, the yard came into view. Stanley was desperate for freedom and made his needs clear as he tugged on the leash and whined in an effort to reach the expansive and lush lawn spread in front of them.

The sight was one Anne never took for granted. An acre of green grass that rivaled any golf course stretched all the way from the house to a border of dense trees.

"Wow, that's quite a yard. How do you get the grass so green?" he asked.

"My aunt spent years cultivating just the right mixture of seed and fertilizer. She used to mow it with a riding mower herself. Now we pay a local kid to take care of it. But this yard is her pride and joy."

"All this is your property?"

She nodded. "On the right we're bordered by those apple trees and lilac bushes." She pointed left and smiled. "That old barn is on the property line to the left."

"No fence?"

She scoffed. "Would you fence in this beauty? We don't have any close neighbors on this side of the road, except an occasional family of deer, so why bother?"

"Good point," he said, suddenly frowning in thought.

When he shifted his stance Anne glanced down at his walking boot. "How's the ankle?"

"Annoying."

"Then I imagine it would be a waste of time for me to mention you should be taking it easy for the first twenty-four to forty-eight hours until the swelling goes down."

"You would be correct."

Anne resisted a smile. Stubborn. That hadn't changed, either.

Stanley's whining became urgent and this time his tugs on the leash were accompanied by low groans of impatience. "Okay to let him run? He can barely stand being on this leash."

"I don't blame him. Of course. Let him have some fun."

Matt held both crutches with one hand and knelt to release the leash. Immediately, Stanley shot forward, nearly knocking Matt off his feet. The crutches dropped to the ground and he pitched forward.

Anne grabbed the tail of Matt's shirt, yanking

him back from a certain fate with the ground, as he, too, struggled for his balance.

"Whoa. Thanks," he said as he righted himself.

When she picked the crutches up from the ground and handed them to him their hands brushed. She nodded, her face warming at the brief touch.

For minutes they both stared quietly at Stanley, a diversion from the awkwardness of the moment. The Lab raced down to the woods, then ran in circles, barking as he chased a bird that soared across the clear blue summer sky overhead.

"That's one happy dog," Anne commented.

"We're renting a house in town with only a small patch of grass."

"I wish we had a dog to take advantage of this yard."

"Why don't you?" he asked. "There are plenty of animals waiting to be rescued and loved at local shelters. That's where we got Stanley."

"It's not that simple. I have a challenging work schedule. I'm constantly on call to back up my team."

"That's the nice thing about a dog. Forces you to go home at the end of the day, because you know they're depending on you."

She mulled his words. "I'll take that under consideration."

"Good. I mean it," he responded.

Stanley stopped running and began to roll over

and over in the grass. Anne couldn't help but laugh at his antics.

"Do you suppose it's true that there aren't any fleas at this elevation?" Matt asked.

"You grew up in Four Forks. Shouldn't you know the answer to that?"

"I've never had a dog before."

She shook her head. "There's a new vet in town. Maybe you should ask."

He nodded. "Good idea."

Anne turned and pointed to the back of the house. "Aunt Lily and Claire will be on the sun-porch or the deck. There's a stone path behind the rose garden that leads to the gazebo. Plenty of shade if you take your dog there."

"Thanks. I'll do that."

"Um, Matt, I suggest you take your time out here."

He frowned in question.

"I think it would be best if my time with Claire is one-on-one for now."

"My presence is a problem?" His eyes narrowed in challenge.

"What I'm saying is that I think your daughter has a lot going on in her head right now. It's normal for her to be confused. And angry."

"What? Angry? She hasn't been angry. I only wish she'd show emotion."

"I've been where Claire is. Trust me. She's angry, all right. If she's reaching out to a stranger for help when she's hit rock bottom, then she's very needy, as well. How long has it been since she lost her mother?"

"Six months. But her mother had been sick for almost a year. Claire was living with the local pastor's family for some time. They tracked me down about six weeks ago." Matt paused. "Fact is, I, um...I didn't even know I had a daughter."

Her head jerked back in surprise. "You just met Claire?"

He nodded. "Yeah."

Anne swallowed, trying to fit all the pieces of the timeline together. There were too many questions that she didn't have the courage to ask right now because the answers were something she wasn't ready to deal with.

"For the record, all I want is what's best for Claire," Matt said. "Tell me what to do and I'll do it. I'll do anything I have to do to ensure she gets better."

"Her world is chaos right now. If I can provide a safe place for her emotionally, then I'll be able to encourage her to participate in her care."

"Okay. Sure." Matt cleared his throat. "Sorry. I didn't mean to sound so defensive before." He raised a hand in gesture. "Look, Anne, I want to apologize for all this."

"This?"

"Inviting ourselves to your home. Barging into your life. It wasn't my idea."

"I realize that. But I like your daughter and, as I said, if this will encourage her to take an interest in her health, then it's a win-win. Right?"

"It seems to me that I'm getting more out of the deal than you are."

Anne nodded to the back of the house where her aunt and Claire now sat outside on the deck in oversize wicker rockers.

"Aunt Lily is thrilled to have company. I haven't seen her so excited in a long time. Most of her friends have either passed away, are unable to drive or are in a residential care facility in Alamosa. She gets a monthly visit from the Paradise Women's Auxiliary, and occasionally goes to Alamosa, but most of the time she's bored. This is a real treat."

"If you say so, but I can't help but think that your arm was twisted."

"I can assure you that it was my decision. I'm not easily persuaded to do what I don't want to do, and I'm happy to do this for Claire."

"Right. For Claire." He cleared his throat. "So you don't find this whole situation awkward?"

"Excuse me?"

He stopped walking. "Anne?"

She was forced to look him at him. The blue eyes were unwavering as they searched her face.

"How long are you going to continue to ignore the elephant in the room?" he asked quietly.

Releasing a breath, Anne stared straight out

toward the faded wood of the old barn, imagining herself anywhere but here right now. "I'm hardly ignoring anything," she said, her voice harsher than she'd planned.

She heard his sharp breath before he spoke.

"Shouldn't I be the one harboring a resentful attitude?" he said.

"Is that how I sound? I'm sorry. I don't mean to be short." She, too, took a calming breath. "I want you to know that I find this just as awkward as you do, Matt, probably more so. I keep trying to remember that we were kids back then. We're adults now. We've moved on."

"Moved on. Is that what we grown-ups have done?"

"Yes. Of course."

"No regrets, huh?"

She sighed, suddenly weary. "Is this really the time to discuss the past?"

"If not now, when?"

She faced him again. His jaw was set as if he was biting back words.

"What do you want from me, Matt?"

"Maybe a few answers. Closure."

"All this time and you haven't had closure?" She looked pointedly across the lawn to where Claire now stood on the steps, her gaze on them, waiting.

"Isn't your daughter evidence that you closed the door on your past a long time ago?"

He winced. "Claire was conceived during a

period when I was hurting and confused. Her mother and I were passing strangers. That wasn't a time in my life I'm proud of."

Anne looked away, not sure she wanted to hear any more and, at the same time, knowing she'd asked for this.

"All I'm saying is that I'd like some time to talk. Don't you think maybe you owe me that much?"

"Owe you?" She shook her head. "I'm not keeping score. The only thing I know for certain is that we have the same goals right now. That's your daughter's health. You and I can talk if you insist. However, not until Claire is on the road to recovery."

"Fair enough," he returned. "I'll hold you to that."

Anne nodded. Of course he would, and maybe she did owe him that much, though she wasn't brave enough to admit he was right just yet.

Anne's words rang in Matt's ears as he moved cautiously on his crutches to the farthest area of the yard where Stanley sat at the base of a tree, watching a squirrel.

Isn't your daughter evidence that you closed the door on your past a long time ago?

She'd hit him right at his most vulnerable point. He shook his head. There was no way to adequately explain the pain he'd been in ten years ago without making his daughter's conception sound like a mistake.

And she wasn't a mistake.

Claire was a beautiful and unexpected blessing in his life. A gift he discovered much too late.

The only mistake was his turning from God in a moment of weakness. He'd thought that nothing else could sting worse than his own self-loathing. He was wrong. Anne had cut him to the core, making him forget for a minute that the Lord had long ago forgiven him for those particular sins.

He eased down onto one of the stone benches that had been placed strategically along the perimeter of the yard and next to overflowing urns of seasonal red and yellow flowers.

"Come on, buddy, leave the squirrel alone."

Stanley whined and then turned away, only to bury his nose in a container of bright blossoms and nuzzle the blooms with his head.

"Yeah. Leave the flowers alone, too. Let's try not to get Anne any more irritated than we have to right now."

Matt stood and hooked the leash to the dog's collar before gently urging the Lab toward the hard dirt path beyond the apple orchard.

They followed a well-used trail for a distance, Matt resting on his crutches at intervals until the lake came into view. His ankle ached, but he ignored the pain.

Leaning against a tree trunk, he gazed out

through the thick perimeter of trees and untamed woodland brush at Paradise Lake. The area was a man-made oasis that had been created in the mountain town. The unexpected beauty stunned Matt every time he was here.

The water sparkled, almost effervescent in the July sun. A few homes had already been completed not far from the water's edge and boasted short piers and docks where small, colorful boats bobbed in the summer breeze.

To the left were boxy summer rental cabins and rustic condos that had been completed in the past few years.

Across the lake, construction had begun on the Paradise Lake Project, a small community of duplexes and cottages that would increase the tourist trade to Paradise and hopefully put his company on the local radar for even more future projects.

Construction equipment noise filled the normally quiet morning even though Manny, his partner and site boss, was still recovering in the Paradise Hospital.

Thinking about Manny, Matt pulled out his cell, punched in the familiar numbers and grinned when his longtime friend answered.

"When are they discharging you?" Matt asked.

"This afternoon, if I play nice. Delia says she'll let me come home if I promise not to scare her like that again."

"How do you feel?"

"Good. It only hurts when I laugh. Those ribs will take a while to heal, but it's amazing what a blood transfusion will do for a guy. I feel like a new man."

"Right." Matt chuckled. "I want you to take it easy. I've got everything under control."

"Sure. I heard. You approved overtime for Saturday. What are you thinking?"

"I'm thinking that we've got to make up the lost time from yesterday while the weather is good."

"Think we'll still come in under budget?" Manny asked.

"If we can get things rolling on the road construction, we'll be looking good."

"So how's Claire? Delia feels really bad about what happened. She figures you're really mad at her."

"Wasn't Delia's fault. In fact everything worked out for the good. Claire is getting the care she needs and we're on track to managing her disease."

"What's the plan?"

"She's with the nurse now," Matt said.

"So you're still at the hospital?"

"No, but don't ask me where I am. You wouldn't believe me if I told you."

"Try me."

Matt turned around to look at the path behind him. "I'm at Anne Matson's house."

Manny sputtered and coughed. "Whoa. What is this, some sort of cruel joke? Cruel for you, at least."

"I wish. She's working with Claire. Diabetic education. Teaching her about her glucose monitor and insulin, and her diet."

"Anne is a nurse?"

"Yeah. Claire met her in the ER yesterday."

"How come I didn't see her?"

"You were out of it until they moved you upstairs to a room. Claire pretty much held me hostage on this situation. Anne or nothing. I didn't have a choice. She is one stubborn kid."

"Not unlike her father." Manny laughed. "The irony of this situation hasn't escaped me."

"Me, either. Twenty-four hours later and my life has been turned upside down and Anne is right in the middle of everything again."

"Matt, you don't still have feelings for her, do you? Come on, not seriously."

"Two days ago I would have said no way. Today, things have changed and I don't know what I have."

"Be careful. You really went off on the deep end last time Anne walked out of your life."

"Don't remind me. Right now, I'm confused about everything."

"You know the answer to that better than I do. Pray, buddy. Pray. That's the bottom line."

"I will. And, Manny, there's one more thing."

"What's that?"

"Anne's house. It's on the list."

There was silence on the phone. "Are you sure?"

"Oh, yeah. I pulled out the plans."

"Does she know that we're doing the demo?"

"I'm guessing not. She hasn't said a thing and that makes no sense. It's as though she doesn't know what's going on."

"You gotta tell her, then."

"No way." Matt ran a hand through his hair. "I can't be the bad guy in this scenario."

"Tell her. It's not your fault. You didn't even know she was living in the house."

"Think she's going to believe that?"

Manny muttered in Spanish and made a sound that registered his frustration. "This isn't going to end well, Matt. You know that."

"Tell me about it. Everything seems easy when you're creating plans on paper, until you realize we're talking about destroying the home of someone you know. And you should see this place."

"Oh, yeah?"

"All kinds of land that spreads forever and no fences. The house has got to be one hundred years old. It's a piece of history."

"We can't change things now. The situation is all about time and money, and we haven't got a lot of either of those particular items."

Matt released a breath. "I know. I know. It would take an act of God to fix this mess."

"I don't rule that out for an answer. We'd better start praying."

"You got that straight."

"Uh-oh, Doc's here to give me a hard time," Manny said. "He must have finished playing golf early."

Matt heard Manny's good-natured laughter and an exchange of voices. Disconnecting, he slid his phone into a pocket and walked slowly back to the house with Stanley by his side.

He shook his head as he crossed the lawn with the Lab at his side. Manny was right. This wasn't going to end well.

A soft breeze stirred the summer air and a young girl's laughter reached Matt from the house ahead.

Claire.

He'd never heard his daughter laugh before.

Gripping his crutches, he stood very still, humbled by the sound.

"Merciful Lord, forgive me for my mistakes. I turn everything over to You. I want to make my daughter happy, Lord."

Chapter Five

"Anne, did you remember to pick up my cookies at Patti Jo's?"

"You must have smelled me coming, Aunt Lily. I have them right here." Anne placed the white box on the end table in the living room. "And how could you think I could I forget? You've gotten two large cookies from Patti Jo's Café and Bakery every Tuesday since the shop opened six years ago. She was finishing up a wedding cake when I went in."

"Oh? For whose wedding?"

"I don't know, but you should have seen the cake. It was like something out of a magazine. Beautiful sugar flowers decorated the outside. And the inside had a layer of lemon."

"Sounds lovely. We can have her make one exactly like it for your wedding."

"My wedding?" Anne chuckled. "Am I getting married?"

"Soon enough, dear. Soon enough."

Anne shook her head and dismissed the comment. "Oh, Patti Jo said to tell you they were freshly made this morning, and she put extra chocolate chips in just for you."

"Isn't she a dear?"

"Yes. She is."

It didn't take much to make her aunt happy. Sitting in her favorite chair, surrounded by her favorite things, was all she wanted. She required so little of Anne, and had given so much to her for twenty-some years. The few times Anne was nagged by regret for her solitary life, she pushed the thoughts away.

While her aunt was distracted by the cookies, Anne moved quietly to the stack of mail on the table. Sifting the obvious junk mail to the bottom, she briefly skimmed the utility statement. More bills. She thought she'd paid everything for the month already.

With her aunt's pension and her salary, they were making ends meet. Though there certainly wasn't much left over, except for needed house repair. She pulled out an official-looking envelope sent by certified mail and turned it over.

Aunt Lily had signed for the letter, but hadn't opened it. That was odd. The return address was the Town of Paradise administrative building. Slipping her fingers beneath the edge, she tore open the letter.

The Town of Paradise wanted to…they wanted to buy the house?

Anne released a small panicked gasp as she continued to read. Her tongue became dry and she could barely swallow. When her knees wobbled, she sank into a dining-room chair.

Was this some sort of mistake?

A secondary road to the new lakeside development.

Construction would commence thirty days after she signed the release. If she failed to sign the release, the town would be forced take legal action. Development was good for the town, the letter pronounced.

Yes. She agreed. Of course. She loved Paradise. But her house? The house was her last thread to family.

Were improvements to the town also good for her and her aunt? Moving would only add to Lily's diminishing mental status.

She glanced around the dining room. How could anyone destroy this amazing beauty anyhow? Why, the kitchen had authentic punched-tin ceilings and oak cupboards. In every room the original architecture had been lovingly cared for. It was a house meant to stand for generations and generations.

What generations? You're the last of the family, a small nagging voice in her head whispered. *You are it, Anne.*

No matter. This was her home. Lily would be devastated.

She stared at the offer. It was decent, she supposed. Her gaze turned to the tall windows at the back of the dining room.

What about the rose garden? The roses themselves had been carefully tended by Lily, and now Anne, for more years than she could remember.

Across from the vine arbor, rows of fragrant vintage blooms exploded with vibrant color, their faces turned upward to greet the partial exposure of the afternoon sun. She silently repeated the names of each variety as she sought to calm her mounting panic.

Grandiflora, tea roses, English roses and damask roses…

It was a road. Couldn't they build the road somewhere else?

Question after question slammed into Anne.

Where would they live? Was there enough money for whatever they needed to do if they left this house?

Biting her lip, she stared at the stamped date on the letter.

Third and final notice?

How could that possibly be? What had happened to the first and second notices?

Anne turned to her aunt whose head bobbed with delight at the commercial for laundry soap.

Aunt Lily.

Some days Lily's mind was her worst enemy. One thing was clear. The new medications weren't helping her Alzheimer's.

Obviously her aunt was hiding mail again.

They'd lost a huge window of time and possibly the advantage.

A constant throbbing slammed against Anne's temples as the blood surged through veins, blurring her vision for a moment.

"Aunt Lily, I'm going out to cut roses."

"All right, dear."

Anne pushed out the French doors to the deck and sank into the wicker chair. At her feet was the cutting basket with shears and gloves. But instead of cutting roses, she read the rest of the letter over and over, again and again.

She reserved the right to appear at a meeting with the Paradise town council in two weeks to petition.

Her mind raced. The mayor. A call to his office might help. Yes, that's what she'd do. She glanced at her watch. Unfortunately it was well after business hours.

It was probably better to plead her case in person, anyhow. After all, Aunt Lily had sat on the town council as an elected member-at-large for a long time. Aunt Lily had once been the heart and soul of the community she'd gladly served. Shouldn't that count for something?

And what about the house itself? The Victorian was more than a century old. One of, if not, the oldest home in Paradise. A spark of hope stirred within her. Perhaps she could file for historic landmark preservation status?

Anne stood and paced back and forth across the faded planks of the deck, debating her options. Thirty days put her at the end of next month. This was the final notice and that deadline was moving toward her like a runaway train. One month to save the house. Could she do it?

If ever she needed divine intervention, the time was now. *Oh, Lord,* she whispered, *show me what to do next.*

Matt checked his watch. He was early. Claire had spent the entire Saturday at the Gray home, by Lily Gray's invitation. Anne said to come by around 7:00 p.m. The timing was perfect, enabling him to work at the Paradise site and giving Claire a change from her usual routine.

The moment he opened the truck door, Stanley bounded out and raced toward the yard as though it was his own, sniffing and running around bushes and trees. Matt followed at a much slower pace, walking around the side to the back of the house.

"Anne, are you all right?" Claire's voice floated from the open window to the right of Matt.

"Hmm?"

"I keep talking to you and you don't answer."

"Oh, I'm so sorry. I was thinking. Sometimes I do that when I have a lot on my mind. My aunt always says I'm in my happy place."

"Are you? Is everything okay?"

"I have a bit of a problem I'm trying to sort out. Actually, I need to just turn it over to God and let him take care of it."

Matt froze. Had she gotten the final notice from the town of Paradise? His heart tripped into overtime as his loyalties began to divide on the battleground of his mind. Either way, his future was on the line, personally and professionally.

"My father says that, too," Claire told her.

"Does he?"

"Last Friday he said he had a really big problem he was turning over to God."

"Friday," Anne murmured, her voice distracted. "So you didn't tell me how your week went, Claire."

"It was good. I checked my glucose all day, every day, except in the night. My father did it while I was sleeping."

"And you recorded the results in your journal?"

"Uh-huh."

"Terrific. You're doing an amazing job, you know."

"I am?"

"Absolutely. Remember how we talked about the insulin pump?"

"Uh-huh."

"What do you think about moving to one in a couple of weeks? I think the doctor will approve since you're handling your diabetic care so well. That way you'll be fully trained and ready to go with it before school starts."

"Okay. If you'll still help me."

"Sure, I will."

"Anne?"

"Yes?"

"Am I going to die from diabetes?"

Only silence filled the air. Matt held his breath, waiting for Anne's response.

"Why do you ask that?" Anne finally said. Her voice remained calm and professional. She was obviously skilled at dealing with emotionally charged questions.

"It's a disease and people die from diseases. My mom died from cancer and that's a disease."

"Let me ask you something. If you were in a car and you started the engine and someone gave it a push down a hill would you be driving the car or would the car be driving you?"

"I guess the car would be driving me."

"That's right."

"And if you had your foot on the gas and your hands on the steering wheel. What then?"

Claire giggled. The sound made Matt smile.

"I would be driving the car."

"Think of your diabetes that way. When you

check your blood glucose levels and eat healthy, you're in charge and that's a good thing."

"And I won't die?"

"You know we all die sometime."

"Is Aunt Lily going to die?"

"Aunt Lily's health isn't as good as we'd like it to be."

"Is she going to die?" Claire repeated.

"Someday."

He heard his daughter's softly drawn sigh.

"That's why it's very important to tell people you care for them. Tell them all the time."

"Do you do that?" Claire asked.

"I try to remember to."

The refrigerator door closed.

"When is your father coming to get you?"

"Soon."

"Do you think he'll be hungry or does he cook his own meals?"

"He doesn't really cook. But the church ladies keep bringing food over to our house."

"Yes. I'm sure they do." Anne gave a small chuckle. "Well, you made this chicken, and it's delicious. Do you want to take the leftovers home with you to share with your father?"

"Could I?"

"Of course. And you know what? We can keep a copy of the recipes you like in a note-book. So when we're done learning about your diabetes you'll have your own Claire cookbook to take home."

"I like coming over to your house."

"And I like having you."

"May I come even if you don't need to teach me?"

"We're friends. Friends visit each other. You're welcome any time you like."

"Do you like my father?"

Anne sputtering was the last thing Matt heard. He'd jerked back at Claire's words, triggering a domino effect.

His aluminum crutches slid from beneath his arms.

Matt groaned as the momentum propelled him forward. He crashed against the deck steps at the same moment that the crutches clattered loudly to the ground.

Seconds later the back door was pushed open and slammed against the house when first Anne and then Claire raced outside.

"Matt, are you okay?" Anne's dark eyes widened in concern as she knelt next to him.

"Other than total humiliation, I'm fine," he muttered. He raised his head and his face warmed at the thought of the image he must have provided. To Anne's credit, she didn't even laugh, and he was grateful.

"Can I help you up?" she asked.

Claire grabbed his crutches as he rolled to his backside.

"I think I've got it." He used the wooden rail to push to a standing position and then took his crutches from Claire. He nodded to his daughter. "Thanks."

"What happened?" Anne asked.

"I guess I got distract—"

He looked up at Anne and froze. Though her dark hair was clipped back from her face, a strand had come loose and he nearly reached a hand to tuck it behind her ear. She was dressed down in jeans and a pink T-shirt with some sort of sports logo and, for a moment, he had an image of Anne in college those many years ago. Matt forced himself to look away.

The direction of his thoughts could only lead to setting himself up for pain once again.

He looked toward the backyard. "Is Stanley okay? Gotta keep an eye on that dog. He thinks he can run down to the lake if I turn my head."

"He's running in circles chasing a butterfly. Stanley is fine. What about you?"

Matt straightened. "I'm good."

"Your ankle? Maybe I should check it."

"I'm good," he repeated. The only thing injured was his pride and that wasn't any sort of new diagnosis.

"That step is sometimes a little wobbly. I'm sure that's what happened."

"Or maybe I'm terminally clumsy." He reached down to test the wooden step and sure enough one of the nails was loose on the right side. Matt looked up at Anne. "Good of you to give me an out."

She smiled.

"Have you got a hammer?"

"I do. Right in the kitchen. I'll get it."

He looked at Claire. "All ready to go?"

"I have to get the chicken and my bag."

"Chicken?" Matt murmured.

Claire nodded and gave a shy smile as she went back into the house.

Anne returned with an assortment of hammers in her hands. Two claw hammers, a ball-peen and a crosshead-peen.

"One is all I need."

"I know, but you didn't say which kind."

He gave a small chuckle at her serious expression.

"What's so funny?" she asked. Her brows were knit in an annoyed frown.

Matt stilled, resisting the urge to tell her that he thought it was cute that she had so many hammers. No, it was best to keep things strictly business between them. Better for his peace of mind at least.

Instead of answering her, he shook his head, took a claw hammer and hunkered down to examine the step again. Two hard taps and the nail was firmly back in place, the step secure once again.

"All fixed."

"Thank you," she said.

"Thanks to you and your aunt for all you've done for Claire."

"It's only been a week and yet she's given us much more than I've given her. My aunt seems to have purpose again. I'd like it if Claire could come over next Saturday afternoon and spend the day again."

"I'll ask her, though it's easy to guess that she'll love that plan."

Matt met her gaze. "I need you to know I really mean it," he said. "She's blossomed, thanks to you."

"Claire is an amazing child. You have her mother and God to thank for that. They laid the foundation. I'm merely offering her the opportunity to do what comes natural."

A moment later Claire emerged from the house with a foil-covered dish in her hands.

"What's this?" he asked.

"Baked herb chicken. I made it myself." An expectant expression crossed her face.

"Wow. You're learning to cook, too?" he asked. "I'm impressed."

Claire glowed beneath the praise.

"All part of our nutritional education," Anne

said. "Besides, she's a quick learner. We're going to be done sooner than I thought."

"You said I could still come over," Claire protested.

Anne placed a hand on Claire's shoulder. "That's right. You can. We're friends now. And you know Aunt Lily loves showing you the secrets of the house. She has plenty more left."

"Secrets?" Matt raised his brows.

"There's a secret door that disappears right into the wall," Claire said. Her eyes were bright with excitement.

"Pocket doors," Matt said with a grin. "Pretty cool."

"That's right. I always forget what the official name for them is. I imagine you architects remember all of that."

"We do."

"Well, this house has two pocket doors."

"What other secrets have you discovered?" Matt asked Claire.

"There's an attic room that you can only get to through a closet, and a turret room I haven't seen yet," Claire continued.

"Did Aunt Lily tell you about the hidden passage in the basement?" Anne asked, her face as animated as his daughter's.

Matt could have stood there watching the two of them talk for hours. They got along like old friends and he admitted to himself that he was envious of their bond.

Claire's mouth formed a circle of astonishment at Anne's question. "Really? No, she didn't tell me about that."

"You'll have to act surprised when she does. I don't want to spoil her fun."

"Where is your aunt?" Matt asked.

"She goes to bed around this time."

"It's still daylight."

"Only because it's summer," Anne reminded him. "Keep in mind that she gets up before sunrise to read her Bible and pray."

"Aunt Lily read the Bible to me today," Claire said. "We're memorizing verses."

"What are you memorizing?" Matt asked.

"Psalms. 'Be of good courage and He shall strengthen your heart all ye that hope in the Lord.'"

"Do you know what that means?" He looked at Claire and smiled.

She shook her head. "Not really."

"It means hang in there. If you trust in God, then eventually everything is going to work out."

Claire's face brightened and she turned to Anne. "Did you hear that? God is going to take care of your problem. Everything is going to work out."

The loving smile Anne gave his daughter caused Matt to pause.

"You're right, Claire," she said. "I guess I'm just a little concerned I might not be prepared for exactly how he's going to take care of my problem."

"But it will all work out. That's the important part. You just have to believe that," Claire returned.

Matt smiled at the wisdom in his daughter's words.

"Did you want to talk about your problem, Anne? Maybe I can help."

"No. Claire is absolutely right. The only thing standing between me and moving this mountain is my ability to trust that God can and will for me. I believe He will. Somehow."

"Okay. I'd like to stand in agreement with you on that, as long as you remember that sometimes He uses His people to help each other."

Anne raised her face and looked at him, her eyes questioning. "Are you telling me you know something I don't?" she probed quietly.

"Not at all. I'm only saying that it's been my experience that often we wait for an answer to prayer, when one is already standing in front of us."

Chapter Six

"Three croissants with Black Forest ham, avocado and Brie to go," Anne said to the clerk at Patti Jo's Café and Bakery.

"Wow. That sounds amazing. I'll take two to go, as well."

Anne whirled around at the sound of Matt's voice.

"Not in your scrubs?" he commented.

"I had a meeting at the hospital. Once or twice a month I try to look like a grown-up instead of a kid in pajamas."

"You look like a grown-up for sure."

When Matt's gaze took in her simple navy suit and pumps she found herself looking anywhere but at him. Why should it matter what he thought of her? Why should his assessment make her nervous?

"Join me for a coffee while we wait?" he asked.

"I, um…"

"It's only coffee, Anne, and I want to talk about Claire. Nothing else. For now."

"Yes…then, I guess so. But I only have a few minutes."

He nodded. "I'll get the coffee, you find a table. Okay?"

"I can do that."

She chose a bistro table rather than a booth, which might make their meeting appear intimate. Patti Jo's tables were higher than regular tables with glossy silver edges and red-laminate tops. Red-cushioned stools were tucked beneath. Anne pulled out a stool and put her purse on the one next to her.

As Matt wove through the small café with two mugs in his hands, several people greeted him. He stopped for a minute at a booth to offer a hello to a group of businessmen.

When he finally slid the mugs on their table she couldn't help but comment. "You certainly have gotten to know people in Paradise in a very short time."

"Networking. It's part of the job. Are you surprised?"

"No, of course not."

He poured creamer into his white stoneware mug and thoughtfully stirred. When his gaze met hers, the blue eyes were cold.

"Ten years ago your aunt predicted I'd be in a dead-end job holding you hostage with me."

"That was my aunt. Not me." She lifted the black coffee to her lips and sipped, needing the jolt of caffeine to deal with Matt's accusations.

"If you didn't believe that, then why did you leave?"

"I thought we were just going to talk about Claire."

"Yeah, well, I've changed my mind."

Anne thought for a few seconds before answering. "Matt, you can't possibly understand what it's like to be alone in the world."

"Can't I?"

"I didn't mean…" She paused and regrouped. "My aunt took me in when there was no one else. She'd planned to travel when she retired, to see the world. And instead she remained in Paradise to raise a ten-year-old child. I owed her my loyalty."

"Did you owe her your future?"

"I was eighteen. I still had three years of college left. She wanted me to finish."

"Oh, it wasn't just about finishing your education and you know that. She pulled you out of D.U. so fast, I didn't even get to say goodbye."

"I'm sorry." Anne swallowed. "That's all I can do now, say that I'm sorry."

"Anne, I forgave you a long time ago. But I still need to understand why."

"You haven't forgiven me," she scoffed. "If you had, you wouldn't need anything else from me."

He wrapped his hands around the mug and slowly nodded. "Maybe you're right. Maybe I'm only human."

"Two lunch orders to go?"

Anne looked up at the waitress who stood at their table. "Yes. Thank you."

She slid from the stool and gathered her purse. "I have to get back to work."

"Wait. I still want to talk about Claire," Matt returned. "Please?" he asked when she didn't respond right away, his gaze softening in apology.

"Claire is doing well, Matt. I anticipate her moving to an insulin pump by the end of summer."

"Good. Good."

"I have to get back."

"I'm sorry."

"There's no need to be sorry. You were right. We had to talk about this eventually."

He offered her a sad nod as she turned away.

Minutes later Anne slammed the door of her truck and hurried into the emergency department with the lunches for herself, Marta and Juanita.

"Did you get lost?" Juanita asked from behind the counter.

"No, I ran into…I had to talk to…"

"Well, it must be a man, because I've never seen you so tongue-tied," Juanita continued.

"Matt was at Patty Jo's. He wanted to discuss Claire."

"Claire. Uh-huh."

Juanita grabbed the sack and opened it. She frowned. "Where's my cookie?"

Anne gasped. "Oh, no. I forgot."

"You forget about us and our cookies for a tall, handsome man?" Juanita's hands went to her hips in a stern stance. A moment later she grinned. "Just kidding. I would have done the same thing."

"It was an accident. An oversight."

"Tell that to Marta. She might believe you."

"Believe what?" Marta asked as she approached.

"She had coffee with Mr. Hunky and forgot our cookies."

Marta chuckled. "This might be a good time to ask if I can leave early. I have to swing by the dry cleaner's to pick up my dress for the hospital dinner tonight."

"No!" Anne glanced at the calendar behind Juanita. "Please, tell me that it's not tonight. Not really."

"It is. Did you forget?" Marta asked.

"Of course I did. I'll have to call to get someone to stay with my aunt." She rubbed her forehead. "I've got eight hours. I guess I'll figure it out."

"Anne, are you all right?"

She frowned as she looked at Marta. "Why do people keep asking me that?"

"Maybe because forgetting cookies and appointments isn't like you," Juanita said.

No. They were right. It wasn't like her. Since Matt had come to town everything had become one continuous "not all right." And it could only get worse.

Matt hadn't been able to take his eyes off her. Though the wisdom of age taught him that beauty wasn't as important as heart and soul, he still had to admit Anne Matson was by far the most beautiful woman in the room. In a swirly, deep purple dress she was a vision unlike any he'd ever seen. The skirt moved when she moved and now as she swayed slightly to the music, the fabric danced around her, as well.

He'd watched her minutes before when she was on the dance floor with Doc Nelson—the tall, smooth guy from the ER that she'd insisted wasn't her boyfriend.

If the good doctor had his way Matt was sure he'd be first in line to claim Anne's affection. The thought rubbed him the wrong way, though he had no right to those feelings. Not to mention that a smart man would be wary of the flame after being scorched the first go-around.

Apparently he'd lost a few brain cells since arriving in Paradise, because here he was moving closer and closer to the light that was Anne. He slowly crossed the room to where she stood next to the buffet table, her head tilted to one side as she pondered the hors d'oeuvres.

"Quite a fancy spread, isn't it? Those bacon wraps are tasty. The bacon hides the vegetables on the inside."

Anne whirled around.

"Matt, I didn't know you were going to be here," she finally said. The words were hesitant.

"First Construction is one of several companies bidding for the hospital contract. If the Paradise Lake project goes well, we'll probably get pulled in for this project, as well."

She nodded slowly, as though considering his words. Then her glance swept the room. "Is Manny here?"

"No. He makes me do anything that involves wearing a suit."

"You look very nice. Where are your crutches?"

"I'm a fast healer."

"Does your doctor know?"

"Yeah, he knows that I'm tired of the crutches and the boot."

"That wasn't quite what I meant."

"I've got a support wrap on the ankle. I'm fine." Matt gave a small nod of dismissal. "Now let's change the subject and talk about you."

"Me?" she asked, her voice cautious.

"You aren't mad at me about our discussion earlier, are you?"

"I was never mad."

"Good, then I guess it's okay to say that you look lovely," he said, and easily meant every word. He took a moment to appreciate the dress close up. Only a moment. Any more than that would be dangerous to his well-being.

Anne held her hands together and then unclasped them, her fingers fidgeting.

Did he make her nervous?

"Thank you," she said, her gaze flitting around the room. She ran a hand over the silky-smooth fabric of the skirt of her dress. "I thought it was a nice change from the navy suits and scrubs I usually wear."

"You're right," he said as he fought a hard battle not to stare at the woman and the dress yet again.

This time a bemused smile curved her lips as though she could read his mind and was flattered.

He smiled, as well, but only for about half a second. Then he realized that Manny was right; she needed to know the truth about him and about his involvement in the decision to destroy her home.

Matt cleared his throat, working up courage. "Listen, Anne, there's something you should know about the Paradise Lake construction project."

"Is it something about my house?"

"Yes."

She stared at him, thinking, her dark eyes confused. Then something changed. Her expression became resolute and she held up a palm and met his gaze. "No."

"No-o?" He dragged out the word, waiting for her to continue.

"I don't want to think about that or talk about it tonight. I've turned it over to the Lord an additional ten times today and for a few hours I'm going to do something out of character by relaxing and having fun."

He knew he shouldn't be relieved, but he was. Eventually he'd pay the price for the reprieve she had handed him, though it wouldn't be tonight. No, not tonight. "Well, I can't argue with that," he said.

Matt dared to shoot a glance at the small dance floor to his right, where the band, consisting of mostly Paradise senior citizens, had begun a slow number.

Anne's boss, Dr. Nicholas Evans, the hospital's director, strode toward them from across the room.

"Matt, I see you've met Anne."

"Yes, sir."

"Band sounds great, doesn't it? Why aren't you young people dancing?"

Matt turned to her as the doctor walked away. "You heard the man. Would you care to dance?"

"But your ankle."

"I'm fine. No fancy moves, that's all."

"Well…"

"Your boss pretty much just ordered you to dance."

A tiny smile urged her lips upward and she glanced from him to the dance floor and back again.

Matt was encouraged.

"What do you say?"

She took a deep breath and gave a "barely there" nod of her chin.

She placed her hand in his palm and he did his best not to let her see how the simple act affected him after all these years.

The music required merely a gentle sway and very little real movement. One hand held hers and the other was carefully positioned and lightly placed at the small of her back.

Anne's fingers were gently splayed upon his lapel. Her dark, silky hair skimmed his chin each time she turned her head. Vanilla and flowery shampoo mingled, filling his senses.

He could have stayed like this for a very long time, he realized.

They moved silently for minutes, somewhat stiffly, until he finally felt her relax in his arms.

"This is a nice little get-together," he said.

"Yes. Paradise is known for events like these. Founder's Day. Fourth of July. We especially like holidays."

"Where do you fit into all of this?" he asked.

"'All of this'?" Her head tilted back as she looked up at him, the dark eyes speculative. "Paradise is my home. What do you mean?"

"I mean this hospital. The new emergency department. They'll start breaking ground on that in the fall. Is that your future?"

"Yes, I suppose it is."

"That doesn't sound very enthusiastic."

"No?" She paused for a moment, as though considering her response. "It's funny you should ask me that, because lately I've been trying to figure out exactly that. Where do I figure in the future of the hospital?" A measure of concern filled her eyes. "I haven't even dared to say that out loud until now."

"You've been here how long?"

"Oh, I was a volunteer first, and this has been the only nursing job I've ever had. So it's been a long time."

"Why aren't you happy?"

She shook her head, her gaze registering confusion. "I thought I was."

"Hmm," he murmured.

"What exactly is on your mind, Matt?"

"I'm wondering if it will bother you that I'm staying in Paradise for the duration. I mean if we get the hospital contract, it'll be another year at least.

"Why would that bother me?"

She stopped moving and he nearly tripped.

"Sorry," he said.

"No. My fault." She looked up at him. "Why would it bother me?"

"I'm just checking. Wondering if we can get to a place where we can be comfortable around each other again."

The music ended and Anne stepped back, remorse on her face. "Matt, I'm so sorry. I've been thinking about our conversation at the café and I don't think I've ever really apologized for..."

This time it was Matt who held up a palm. "My turn to say no. We need to discuss the past, but tonight isn't the right time. For this evening let's pretend we're old friends."

"Friends?"

"Yes. That was my plan."

Anne nodded and his heart swelled with hope. It was a good place to begin. To start over.

Remember not the former things, nor consider the things of old.

Yes, Lord, that's exactly right. Did he dare hope? Could he have a future here in Paradise? Why not?

Matt smiled down at the woman in front of him.

Then he remembered her house.

"Let me get this straight. You can't ask him about the house, but you can dance with him?"

Anne slid into her seat next to Marta.

"Dr. Evans practically insisted on it. I only did it to be polite." She adjusted her dress and reached for her iced tea goblet.

"Yes. I can see that." Marta nodded toward the dance floor. "We have a very polite little town. Getting more polite by the minute."

"What are you talking about?"

"The man has danced with every single woman in the room. Except me, of course."

"Has he?" Anne turned her head back to the crowded dance floor. Sure enough, Matt was dancing with Sally-Ann from Paradise's only beauty salon. Suddenly her time with Matt lost its significance. Then she remembered his words from the café.

"I think it's all about networking."

Marta laughed. "Networking? I don't think so. They all *asked* Matt to dance. He's doing a good job, too."

Anne didn't answer. Determined to avoid looking back at him a second time, she sipped her tea. Matt's dance partners were none of her business. None. He was a handsome man, below the age of sixty-five, which made him a rare and precious commodity in Paradise.

After a few minutes Marta reluctantly turned around. "Did you ever get an appointment with the mayor?"

"No, but his secretary said he did want to

speak with me. She suggested I show up early to the town meeting."

"When is that?"

"In two weeks. Remember?"

"Oh, that's right. Well, it gives you plenty of time to talk to Matt."

"Oh, look, Luke Nelson is dancing with your daughter. They look good together."

"Do they?" Marta asked. "I sort of had my heart set on Megan falling in love with Sheriff Sam. The nurse and the sheriff. Sounds perfect to me."

"Sam will never marry. You know that."

"Those wounded types are so attractive. Don't you think?"

Anne laughed. "Maybe you should be writing books instead of being a professional matchmaker."

"I just might do that. After I get my daughter taken care of, of course." She frowned and screwed up her face in deep thought. "Do you think Nelson is marriage material?"

"He's got a steady job and doesn't live with his mother." Anne assessed the doctor. "And as far as doctors go, he treats everyone well."

"You're right. I've seen him at church, too." Marta narrowed her eyes. "I wonder if he likes kids."

Anne couldn't resist a laugh. "Does she know about your plot?"

"Of course not, but she's been a widow for five years now. Those kids need a daddy and she needs someone to share life's adventures with."

"Seriously? 'Share life's adventures'? That sounds like a logo for a dating site." Anne chuckled. "Maybe your daughter likes being single. I like it."

"So you say, though I can tell that you most certainly don't look all that happy to me."

"We weren't talking about me." Anne wiped the condensation from her goblet. "Have you considered letting things play out on their own?"

"Don't be silly, Megan is almost as oblivious as you."

"What does that mean?" This time she turned to her friend, almost afraid of the bluntly honest response she would be certain to receive.

"It means that you probably have no clue that Matthew Clark is still half in love with you."

"Marta, he hasn't seen me in years."

"That has zero to do with anything. Men don't get over love easily. Especially their first love. They tend to talk about the first girl that stole their hearts for years." She sighed and shook her head. "Trust me. Ad nauseam."

Anne laughed. "But that doesn't mean Matt's that way. He's got a lot of resentment inside him and he has every right. I hurt him badly."

"Honey, he's been watching you all night. He may be fighting his feelings, but trust me, the man is definitely not indifferent when it comes to you."

Anne opened her mouth and closed it again as Marta's words reverberated through her.

Was it possible that she was right? Anne was stunned silent and confused at the possibility.

Chapter Seven

What a lousy end to an otherwise enjoyable evening. Anne stood next to her truck, parked at the far end of the parking lot, staring at the rear passenger side where the deflated tire was pointedly illuminated by the streetlight.

"Yeah. It looks flat to me," Matt said.

She turned, half relieved, half terrified to see him again so soon. The light glowed behind him, making him seem almost surreal. But he was real, all right. All six feet and wide shoulders' worth of him. He'd loosened his tie and his hair was mussed and all she could do was stare while asking herself the same question Marta had not long ago. Why had she left such a man?

"Give me your keys, I'll change the tire."

Roused from her reverie, her hands moved to her hips. "I can change a flat tire. I'm not the kind of woman who needs to be rescued."

"Never crossed my mind, princess, but you

aren't exactly dressed for the occasion, and even you can use a little help sometimes."

Her head reared back in surprise. "What did you call me?"

"Um, sorry. Claire says you're a princess and your house is a castle."

"I wish I were."

"That's sort of a princess dress."

She released an embarrassed laugh, knowing his words pleased her. "Is it?"

"Yep."

She glanced down and sighed. Fine. He was right. She couldn't change a flat tire in a "sort of a princess dress."

Matt held out his hand. Anne fished in her purse, pulled out her keys and dropped them into his palm. "Okay, but I want to assist."

He shook his head. "Of course, you do. Why don't you get the owner's manual?"

She nodded.

Matt grabbed tools from under the front seat and pulled the tire from under the truck bed.

"Here." Anne handed him a blanket. "No need for you to get that nice suit dirty."

"You're right." He slipped off his jacket. "I'll take it, thanks." She carefully folded the material and placed it on the driver's seat.

Matt wedged off the hubcap and got to work loosening the lug nuts, grunting as he turned the wrench. "Who tightened these? The Incredible Hulk?"

Anne cleared her throat. "I did."

"You don't know your own strength, do you?"

"As I recall I was pretty cranky the last time I got a flat tire. I didn't have anyone offering to change it for me."

"Remind me not to make you cranky." He stood on the wrench arm with his full weight, finally loosening the first one.

Though guilt plagued Anne, she found herself staring as he rolled up his sleeves a little more, which made his biceps peek out.

Matt Clark had very nice biceps.

He moved to the other lug nuts, each one as difficult as the first. Fifteen minutes later and he was ready for the jack.

She flipped through the pages of the book and began to read. "'Use the jack to lift the vehicle off the ground. Once the jack is secure, jack up the truck until the tire is about six inches off the ground.'"

"What are you doing?" he asked with a groan of disbelief.

"Reading the manual." She glanced down at him before continuing. "'Remove the lug nuts and pull the tire off the truck.'"

"Anne."

"Hmm?"

"I got this."

"You don't want me to read the instructions?"

He pulled the tire off. "No."

"So, what can I do?"

He wriggled the spare onto the truck and lined up the lug nut holes and then lowered the vehicle back to the ground.

"Here. Put the jack in the backseat while I tighten the lug nuts."

When she returned he was standing and there was a large streak of black dirt across his right cheek. Anne reached into the truck and handed him disinfectant wipes.

"Your, um, face has stuff on it."

"You keep hand wipes in your car?"

"I do. You never know when you might need to sanitize your hands."

"Spoken like a true nurse." Matt wiped his face and then his hands.

She held out a plastic bag for him to dispose of the wipes. "Always prepared," he continued.

"Occupational hazard," she said quietly.

But when Matt leaned closer, she wasn't prepared. Not the least bit. This was premature no matter how you looked at it. Yet she found her knees weak as she inhaled the scent of his aftershave along with traces of tire and grease.

He came closer.

Surely not? He wasn't going to kiss her, was he?

She swallowed. Her breath caught.

How would she resist? Like a foolish teenager, she'd dreamed of Matt's kisses long after he'd disappeared from her life.

"Excuse me," he murmured.

"Hmm?"

"I need to grab my jacket from your truck."

"Oh, of course. Sorry." She quickly moved away from the door.

"No problem."

Anne cleared her throat and glanced away, suddenly preoccupied with the scattered pebbles in the road.

He wanted his jacket. Not her. What had she expected?

Nothing like totally humiliating herself with the glow of the streetlight to illuminate her face. Her cheeks were warm, which meant that without a doubt her face was bright red.

"Why don't you go ahead?" he said.

"Hmm?"

"You go ahead," he repeated. "I can follow your truck down the street to make sure everything is okay."

Anne gave a tight nod. "Thank you for changing my flat."

She dared peek up at him.

He smiled.

It would be helpful if he could be a little less handsome and a little more aware of his impact on her. No. Barring complete disfigurement, he'd still be Matt, and the man happened to be humble inside and out.

"Terrific," she mumbled.

"Are you talking to yourself?" he asked.

She was jerked out of her thoughts. "Was I talking aloud?"

Matt nodded.

"I do that sometimes."

"You do?" His expression clearly said that most people did not.

"Another job hazard."

"Okay, then. I guess I'll see you."

"Maybe we could go for coffee again?" she suggested, suddenly reluctant for him to leave.

"I wish I could, but I've got a sitter to relieve. I'm sure you do, too."

"Yes. Right." She opened the truck door further. "Thanks again."

"No problem."

But it was a problem, because the more time she spent around him the more she questioned why she'd left him in the first place.

Matt paid the babysitter; a pleasant teen who worked at the bakery. He moved down the hallway, his steps light. The evening had been exceptional and the perpetual smile on his face since he'd left Anne in the parking lot was proof that his heart was equally light.

He gently knocked on Claire's door.

"Come in."

The door squeaked as he edged it open. She was sitting cross-legged on the floor, in her pajamas, going through a photo album, her back to him.

"How'd it go with the sitter?" he asked.

"Fine."

"Is that fine good or fine you only tolerated her?"

"She let me make that chicken recipe that Anne gave me and we watched a movie."

He inched into the room. Something in her voice still said things weren't really fine at all. In fact, his gut told him there was a real problem brewing.

"Are you okay, Claire?"

She sniffed and nodded, but her long, tawny hair shielded her face from him. As he got closer, and she met his curious gaze, Matt could see the drying trail of tears. Her eyes were red-rimmed and swollen.

"Claire, what's wrong?" Alarmed, Matt crouched beside her, before he realized he had absolutely no clue how to handle a young girl's tears.

"It's almost my birthday." She fought and failed at keeping her voice steady.

A pang of regret slammed into him. He'd totally forgotten her birthday was coming up.

Think, Matt, think. What did the paperwork the attorney gave him say?

"August twenty-first," he burst out. "Next weekend."

"You remembered."

Barely.

"You'll be ten."

She offered him a watery smile of pleasure and wiped at her face with her knuckles.

"What did you and your mother do for your birthday?" he asked as he eased to the floor, stretching out his legs on the oak planks.

"We went to dinner at whatever restaurant I wanted. I got to pick because it was my special day."

"You want to go to a restaurant? Don't you want to have a party with cake and balloons and stuff, and maybe invite some friends from church?"

"That's for babies. I'm not a baby. I want to go to a restaurant and wear a pretty new dress."

"Sure. Sure. We can do that."

"I can have a new dress for my birthday?"

"That, too." Anything. This was his daughter. Claire Griffin Clark could have whatever she wanted.

"Maybe Anne could take me shopping."

Matt froze. He could promise his daughter the world, but he couldn't promise her Anne.

And Anne wasn't going to be there forever.

She had her own life. The day would come when she wouldn't have time for Claire. She'd disappear from his daughter's life just as she had from his.

Somehow he had to get his Claire less dependent on Anne and more dependent on her own father.

"Uh, I don't know if she'll have the time."

"Yes, she does. We're friends."

"I suppose we can ask her."

"Can we invite her to dinner, too?"

"I thought maybe you and I could do something together."

"It's my birthday. I want Anne to come, too."

"S-s-sure," he stuttered. "That's fair. It is your birthday. We'll ask her that, too, but don't be upset if she can't. Anne has an important job and she takes care of her aunt."

"She'll come for me. I know she will."

"So, where do you want to go?"

"Aunt Lily says there's a place in Four Forks that has lava cake. I've never had a lava cake in my whole life."

"Aunt Lily, huh?"

"She said to call her that."

"I see. Well, a lava cake seems like it might not be healthy."

"Anne says I can eat anything I want as long as I monitor my glucose. Lava cake is for special occasions. My birthday is a special occasion. So it's okay."

Matt gave a slow shake of his head. "Well, she's the expert. That's for sure. So if Anne says it's okay, then it's okay."

He turned his attention to the photo album in his daughter's lap. Pictures of Claire and her mother filled the pages.

"May I look at your album?"

Claire nodded.

"Why didn't you and my mom get married?"

"That's one of those grown-up questions that I promise to answer someday."

It had to be someday, because right now he was still sorting out how he was going to explain that he wasn't perfect and more often than he liked, he made mistakes and he, too, had to ask God for forgiveness.

He looked at Claire and then down at the album. She looked so much like her mother.

Emotions he'd ignored for too long rose up and he swallowed hard. All he wanted was to give her back everything she'd lost. His daughter wouldn't live like he did, constantly wondering if he was loved. Claire would always know. He'd make sure of that.

"Are you okay, living here with me and Stanley?"

Claire nodded. "Yes."

"You're sure?"

"Yes."

"Did you meet any friends in vacation Bible school last week?"

"A few. Maybe I'll see them in church."

"Good idea. We need to start going to church regularly." He shook his head in agreement with his own decision. "What else can I do to make things better for you, Claire?"

"I don't know. Things are okay."

"Are they?" Was okay a good place to be for an almost-ten-year-old? He didn't know. His childhood wasn't any sort of benchmark for comparison.

"You don't have to try so hard," she murmured. "I like you."

Matt jerked back slightly at the words. "You do?"

"Yes."

His heart soared. His daughter liked him and he and Anne were friends. Not a bad end to an evening. He didn't resist the silly grin that escaped.

"Do you think you could call me Dad sometime?"

"Maybe." She sniffed the air. "Why do you smell like grease?"

"I changed Anne's flat tire."

"She was at the thing you went to?"

"Uh-huh, and you were right, Claire."

"I was?" Her head moved and she peeked at him with quiet curiosity. "What was I right about?"

"She looked like a princess."

Claire beamed.

"You're going with us?" Anne asked Matt the following Saturday.

"Don't look so surprised."

"I am. You didn't mention you were planning on joining us when you asked me."

"Is that a problem?"

She shrugged. "I don't know. I've never gone dress shopping with a man."

"I'm not a man. I'm her father."

Anne did a double-take before a belly laugh bubbled up from inside her. Her hand went to her mouth immediately, but it was far too late for that. The laugh had burst into the room.

All she could do was clear her throat and attempt to put on a serious face. So far it wasn't working. "Sorry, but, um, that somehow struck me as funny."

He pursed his lips. "Funny ha-ha or I'm funny."

"I don't know. Just funny."

"Maybe it would help if you thought of me as your chauffeur. My idea was that I might learn a little bit more about how to be a parent to Claire if I came along."

"You know you're a good dad, right?"

"I'm trying. The fact is Claire is very dependent on you, Anne, and I want her to turn to me. I'm her father."

Anne stilled at his words. "I hope you don't think I'm trying to usurp your place as parent."

"Not at all. I'm just realizing I need to try harder."

"Okay," she murmured.

"Besides, I'm also going because the nearest mall is Pueblo and that's over two hours away. We can take my truck."

"I have a truck, too."

"Mine is bigger."

Anne shook her head. "Bigger isn't always better."

"With trucks it is."

She gave an exaggerated roll of her eyes. "Okay, fine. But you know you're probably overthinking this whole parenting thing, right?"

"Possibly, but I'm a hands-on guy. Reading books like you do doesn't do it for me."

"Would you like a little advice about our outing today?"

"Sure."

"Shopping with girls involves a lot of walking." She glanced down at his feet.

"Why? You go in and buy the dress and get out."

Anne tried, yet once again laughter erupted.

"Glad you're finding this so amusing. I don't think I've ever heard you laugh so much." Matt pulled open the hall closet and grabbed a pair of sneakers. "These work?"

"They might. But you really have to have the stamina and fortitude for this job."

He narrowed his eyes. "Right. Like working construction doesn't provide me with much stamina and fortitude. I'd flex my big manly muscles for you, but I don't want to tear this shirt."

Anne bit her lip. "Fine. Just don't say I didn't warn you."

He scoffed loudly and looked toward the hall. "Claire, we're ready."

His daughter came into the living room, a puzzled expression on her face. "What do you mean 'we'?"

"I'm going to go, too," Matt said.

Her face reflected pure horror.

"But we're going shopping for a dress and shoes and maybe hair stuff."

"I can keep myself entertained."

Claire looked at Anne.

Anne shot her a weak smile.

"You won't even know I'm around," he murmured.

Anne and Claire exchanged knowing glances that said they fully concurred. Not knowing Matt was around would never be a true statement. Not in a million years.

* * *

Five hours after they arrived at the Pueblo mall, Anne checked her watch as they headed back to the parking lot in search of the truck.

"Maybe I should drive." She peeked at Matt's face as he loaded their packages into the shell-covered back of his pickup. He was doing an admirable job of pretending he wasn't exhausted and in severe pain.

"I'm good. Although I will admit that I never in my entire life would have believed anyone could shop for five hours."

"Matt, you're limping. Maybe you should take an aspirin and I'll drive."

"I don't need an aspirin." He scoffed at the suggestion. "Besides, all sorts of great and wonderful things come from suffering." He cocked his head toward his daughter. "Look at her face."

He was right. Claire's grin was two miles wide. Her eyes were round and sparkling with joy.

Anne handed him a hot-pink shopping bag by the beribboned handle. "You're a good father."

"Am I? Seems like I don't know what I'm doing most days and the rest of the time I'm just playing catch-up."

"I believe most parents feel that way a large percentage of the time."

"Hmm. If that's the case, why do people keep having kids?"

"I'm probably not the right person to answer that question."

"You ever think about having kids?"

Startled, Anne nearly dropped the beverage cup in her hand. "Not much anymore."

"It's not like you're too old, you know."

"Yes, but…" She paused, hoping beyond reason that if she didn't answer he might change the subject.

Awkward silence stretched between them and she knew it was because they were both thinking the same thing. They could have had a child. Together. If they had remained married.

"But what?" he finally said. "Biological clock aside, you could even adopt as a single mother."

"I could. The truth is, Matt, I haven't had time to give the subject a lot of thought lately."

"The trouble with that line of reasoning is that by the time you do have time, it will be too late."

"I appreciate your concern. Thank you."

"Hmm. Why do I doubt that?" he murmured.

Matt moved to the passenger side of the truck to open the back door for Claire and the front for her. As he did, a double stroller passed by the rear of the car next to them. Anne turned to glance at the toddlers that were strapped in and smiled at the irony.

"Anne?"

She looked up. "Sara!" She reached out to hug

her good friend Sara Rogers. "Ben, good to see you, too."

Anne turned to Matt and Claire. "Sara and Ben, this is Matt Clark and his daughter Claire. Ben and Sara are doctors from Paradise Hospital. They work our remote traveling bus that goes into the rural areas of the valley."

Matt reached out to shake both of the Rogers's hands, a smile on his face. "Great to meet you." He glanced down at the babies. "Twins? Now that's the way to do it, don't you think, Anne?"

Anne offered an anemic laugh, her face hot with embarrassment. "We were just talking about…" She waved a hand as she realized she was digging deeper and deeper into a hole she could never find her way out of alone. "Oh, never mind."

Sara chuckled. "Now you've got me curious."

"Oh, just one of those random conversations," Matt said.

Sara and Ben exchanged glances and smiled indulgently at them like an old married couple.

"Good to see you two and the girls," Anne said.

"We were going to stop for dinner before heading home. Did you want to join us?" Ben asked.

"We just ate at Los Très." Anne held up her go-cup as evidence. "But, thanks. Maybe another time."

"You know, we'd love that. We don't know

many couples our age," Sara said, a wistful tone in her voice. "I will for sure call you."

Matt held the door for Claire and closed it carefully. Then he opened Anne's and leaned close as she got in. "We've been promoted to a couple," he whispered.

"I'm sorry. I thought it was easier to let it go."

"Don't be sorry. I'm flattered."

"Are you? Really?" She turned and her face was inches from his.

"Yeah. Really," he said softly.

Her heart tripped as his warm breath touched her face and she saw the truth in his eyes. Anne licked her lips, grateful for Claire in the backseat.

She and Matt a couple? Anne hadn't dared to let her mind travel down that particular road. They'd barely gotten to friends yet. Yesterday was long gone. They had moved on. Or had they?

Her aunt's world was one where trust was in God and not in mere mortal man. Where a solitary life was safe.

Unfortunately it was also very lonely. That brought her full circle to the house. Why was she struggling to save a house where she would spend the rest of her life alone anyhow?

The more she was around Matt and Claire, the more confused she became. Or maybe she was becoming *less* confused, as what she wanted became clearer. But that absolutely terrified her because she didn't know if she had the courage to reach for it.

Chapter Eight

Claire's nose was practically pressed flat against the glass of the pickup's back window as they drove down the main thoroughfare of the small town of Four Forks, Colorado. This past week she'd been happier than Matt had ever seen her and the extra advantage was the two Saturdays in a row that he and his daughter had gotten to spend with Anne.

This was good, but also worrisome. He'd like his daughter to show as much enthusiasm for spending time with him. Was that possible?

"Four Forks is even smaller than Paradise," Claire murmured with awe as they passed a fountain in the downtown area.

"Tell me about it," Matt said over his shoulder. "One stoplight and no movie theater. Blink and you've finished touring the town. All I ever thought about for eighteen years was leaving,"

"You grew up here?" his daughter asked. "In Four Forks?"

"I did."

"Where is your house?"

"Oh, we moved around a lot."

"Where are your parents?"

"You know, I don't exactly know where my mother is and my father passed away a long time ago."

"So I have another grandma somewhere?"

"Somewhere covers a lot of space, Claire. I have no idea where my mother is."

"I don't understand. How can you not know where your mom is?"

"You didn't know where I was for a long time. Sometimes life gets complicated. That's all."

Matt watched her in the rearview mirror. She leaned back against the leather upholstery, thinking for moments. "You grew up in Paradise, right, Anne?" she finally asked.

"Yes. I moved there when I was your age."

"When your parents died?"

"Uh-huh. I've lived there ever since, in my aunt's big old house."

"Four Forks is pretty close to Paradise. Did you ever meet my father?"

"As a matter of fact, your father and I knew each other in college."

His eyes searched Anne's across the space of the truck and he saw the moment she began to remember the first time they'd met. Campus mailboxes; he was trying desperately to open his combination lock only to realize he was at the wrong mailbox.

Anne smiled and turned to look out the window.

"Did you ever go out on a date with my father?" Claire asked.

"Look. There's the restaurant," Matt interrupted. He eased the truck into a parking spot, praying the conversation would neatly detour, as well. They'd stumbled into the "it's complicated" territory long enough. No use spoiling the day by making them all uncomfortable.

Besides, today was all about Claire, not him and Anne, and he was determined to keep the focus on his daughter.

"Where? I don't see any restaurant," Claire asked.

"See that lodge-looking building? That's the place. Pine Lodge. We've got reservations for five o'clock. So we're right on time."

He jumped from the truck to open first Anne's door and then Claire's.

Claire skipped ahead of them, pausing occasionally on the sidewalk to shyly admire her reflection in the shop windows, twirling to see the dress's skirt float around her.

"It's a beautiful dress. You did good, Anne."

"Claire knows what she wants. I was a little

surprised. She always wears hoodies and jeans. That dress is all femininity. Just look at those ruffles."

"Mmm-hmm. Looks like you got a new dress, too," he said. It took significant determination not to stare.

She glanced down at the red print dress she wore with a little red sweater.

"Claire's enthusiasm was very contagious. Generally I am not a big shopper."

"You look beautiful. You should wear scrubs less and dresses much more often."

Her face pinked and she smiled. "Thank you."

Matt held the door for them as they entered the lodge restaurant. "You notice how everyone is looking at us, wondering how I got so lucky to be escorting two beautiful women to dinner," he said for their ears only.

"Aunt Lily calls that honeyed talk," Anne whispered to Claire.

The little girl giggled.

Anne pointed to a plaque on the wall, her face bright with excitement. "Look at this. The lodge portion of the facility is listed in the National Register of Historic Places. It was built in 1926 as a boarding house for the mill workers in the nearby mill. Why, my home is older than this."

"How old is your house?" Matt asked.

"One hundred and nine years old. Goodness,

this gives me hope my house will be approved when the paperwork is reviewed."

"I didn't know you applied," he murmured.

"Too late, it seems, but you never know. I did put everything in God's hands, right?"

"Right. Right." As he said the words Matt began to mull them and consider once again how he could help Anne save her house, because he knew that losing that Victorian lady would certainly put a divide between them.

Once they were seated, Matt leaned over to Claire. "You checked your glucose before we left the house, right?"

Claire nodded. "Not too high…"

"Not too low." He followed her example.

Anne smiled and joined in. "But just right."

Matt chuckled at their inside joke.

The waiter brought the menu and they spent another ten minutes laughing and talking while they decided what to order.

As they waited for their meal, Anne reached into her purse. "I almost forgot your birthday present."

Claire's eyes widened and her shoulders scrunched in an expression of pure excited delight as the small silver box with a silver ribbon was placed in front of her.

"For me?"

Anne narrowed her eyes, glanced around the

room as if searching. "You're the only birthday girl here."

Claire laughed at her antics. There was no savoring the moment as she opened the wrapping, until the box was free of trimmings. Inside, on a bed of white cotton, lay a sterling-silver, vintage charm bracelet. A diabetes alert charm in red and silver hung from the dainty chain.

"Oh, it's so pretty."

"They sure have changed Medical Alert bracelets, haven't they?" Matt asked.

Anne nodded.

"Is this like what Aunt Lily wears around her neck?"

"Not exactly. Hers has a little panic button. She can press it if she falls and someone will be sent to help her."

"I didn't know that," Claire remarked. She held up the bracelet to Anne. "Will you put it on me?"

"Sure," she returned.

Claire admired her wrist where the bracelet hung. "So pretty."

"It is," both Anne and Matt said at the same time.

Her gaze met his and she smiled, melting the edges of his heart. For tonight, at least, it seemed as if they were in their own little world, and he liked it that way.

"I guess maybe I could give you my present

now, as well," he finally said to his daughter. "I mean if you want it."

She gave a small gasp. "Another present? But you already bought me my dress and shoes."

"Oh, that's just routine girl stuff." Matt, too, pulled a small jewelry box from his pocket. It was smaller than the box Anne had given Claire, with a red ribbon around a white leather box.

"Another jewelry box." Claire grinned.

"Like minds," Matt murmured, his gaze meeting Anne's once again.

Claire fingered the small white box and played with the ribbon.

"Aren't you going to open it?"

"Yes." This time Claire gently removed the bow and slowly pulled open the hinged box. Inside, a silver heart locket with a chain rested on white velvet. She looked up at him, chewed her lower lip then inhaled and swallowed.

"The locket opens."

Claire's breath caught when she flipped open the locket and turned the case around toward her to examine the inside photo. "Oh, it's my mom." She held it out for Anne to see. "It's my mom."

"Beautiful," Anne said. When she smiled her eyes became suspiciously moist.

Matt was totally unprepared when Claire placed her napkin on the table, eased from her chair and threw her arms around his neck as she kissed his cheek. "Thank you, so much, Daddy."

She'd finally used the D word.

He was forced to look away as the realization of how far he and his daughter had come shook him to his core.

When he turned back Anne was talking to Claire and he couldn't help the direction of his thoughts. If the good Lord could perform this miracle with his daughter, then certainly He could get Matt to the place where forgiving Anne wasn't just words. Could he put his pride aside to seek a second chance with Anne?

Would she be open to one?

The thought terrified him as much as it excited him.

When dinner was served, things moved quickly as Claire became very impatient for her promised treat; the dessert that Lily Gray had suggested was fitting for a birthday girl. There was little discussion once the sweets cart appeared at their table.

"Lava cake. That's the one."

An elderly woman walked by the table and paused, her gaze lighting on first Matt and then Anne. "Excuse me for interrupting, but I've been watching your family. I can see it's your daughter's birthday. She's such a lovely girl. You two have done a fine job raising her." She turned to Claire. "Happy birthday, dear."

Claire beamed. "Thank you."

When the woman left, Claire leaned close to

Anne on her elbows and whispered behind her hands. "She thought you were my mother."

"I'm sorry. Does that upset you?"

"No, because I know my mother would really have liked you. Just like I do."

"Oh, Claire, that's so sweet." Anne's eyes once again were bright with moisture.

Matt also found himself overcome with emotion. The constant what-ifs of the time lost between him and Anne continued to spin through his thoughts.

He'd promised himself today was all about Claire, yet he couldn't ignore the woman across from him or his confused feelings for her.

When the waitress brought their check he turned to Anne. "Do we need to get you back home soon? Is Lily alone?" he asked.

"Oh no, she goes down to Alamosa a few times a month to visit with a friend in a retirement community. They came and got her today."

"Is she thinking of moving there?"

"Never. She loves to visit, but she's determined to stay in her house."

"Did you know that Anne's great-great-grandfather built that house? Aunt Lily's grandpa," Claire commented. "He put that white stone on the fireplace."

"White marble," Anne corrected. "From Marble, Colorado. The same stone that's in the capitol building in Denver."

"I didn't know that."

No, he had to admit he hadn't considered the home's emotional history before now. He'd merely designed the best ingress and egress to the lake community. No emotions involved. Simple pragmatics. While he'd always understood the historical connection and value of housing structures, today's discussion about his heritage caused him to consider the emotional aspect. Roots and family tree were absent from his life, but not from Anne's.

Was there something he hadn't thought of? Something he needed to do that could change everything. Could it be the Lord was nudging him to dig deeper. To find a way to save Anne's home?

It seemed an impossible task.

Anne reached for her chiming cell phone and offered a groggy hello. She blinked but her room remained dark. Either she was dreaming or it really was the middle of the night.

"Anne, I'm sorry to bother you, but Claire's blood glucose level is registering low."

"Low? How low?"

"No reading. Just low." Matt's voice was taut with fear.

Her eyelids popped open and she sat up in bed, instantly awake. "Is she responsive?"

"Yes."

"And you? Are you okay?" she asked him.

He released a breath. "Trying to be okay is the best I can do right now."

"Matt, you can handle this."

"Can I? I'm starting to think I'm the last person who should be handling this."

"You know the drill. Give her a box of juice and test her glucose level in ten minutes."

"Can you come over?"

"Of course. Tell me where you live."

He rattled off an address in downtown Paradise.

"I'll be there in fifteen minutes. Call me back if you need to."

"Okay. Thanks."

Anne went to peek on Lily and then realized she was still out of town. She brushed her teeth and pulled on jeans and a sweatshirt and then grabbed her keys. Running a hand through her hair would have to suffice as a fix for her bed head.

There was no traffic in Paradise except one lone patrol car parked on the edge of town. The town's only deputy waved at her from his marked vehicle. She waved back and checked her speedometer, easing up on the gas pedal. No use breaking the law.

Matt could handle things, despite his thoughts to the contrary. She understood that this was his first diabetic crisis and she would be on hand for moral support, but she was confident that he'd do everything right. Matt was a very smart man.

His little rental house was only a few blocks off Main Street. He was right; it was a tiny cottage with a postage-stamp-size yard illuminated by a trail of solar-light stakes. She could hear Stanley barking from inside the house as she approached the front walk.

The door swung open and Matt stood behind the screen with the excited dog pushing his way around him in an effort to see who had arrived.

Matt's jeans were wrinkled and his T-shirt was on inside out. The relief that was evident on his face spoke volumes and she was flattered that he trusted her expertise.

"How's she doing?" Anne asked.

"Better." He held open the screen. "The meter popped up into a low normal range with the juice."

"What do you think happened?" Anne asked.

"I don't know. Maybe she ate less than she thought she did. She was sniffling earlier after dinner. Did you notice? Could be she's getting a cold."

"Good evaluation, Dad. All good answers. But did you ask her?"

"No. I didn't want to come off as the bad guy. I waited for you to get here."

"Aha, you want me to be the bad guy." Anne

chuckled. "You know that eventually you're going to have to take over that role. I won't be around every time her sugar drops."

"Yeah. I know. More than you realize."

Anne frowned at his words. "May I see her?"

He nodded and she followed him down a short hallway to Claire's room. A soft light glowed from a bedside lamp. Claire sat up in bed with at least a dozen stuffed animals around her. Matt had done a nice job transforming the little room into a girly retreat with pale pink walls and matching décor.

"I see you're having a slumber party. You know I've never been to one before."

"Never?"

"No," Anne said with a sigh. "Aunt Lily wouldn't let me out of her sight overnight." She glanced around. "Who are all these guys?"

Claire smiled. "This is Shorty." She lifted a pink bear and then pointed toward the rest of the lineup. "I haven't really named the rest of them."

"How are you feeling?" Anne asked.

Claire shrugged.

"May I see your journal?"

The girl opened the bedside drawer and took out the notebook and handed it to her.

"Everything here looks good, except that… hmm, I don't see your bedtime snack."

Claire's lips became a thin line.

"Maybe I missed it?"

Anne turned a page slowly.

"No. I forgot. I ate so much at my birthday dinner..."

"And you dosed adequately. Your glucose levels were fine two hours after dinner." Anne set the journal aside. "Who's driving the car, Claire?" she asked gently.

"I am."

"That's right. Where are your snack attack cards?"

She pointed to her pink backpack.

Matt reached for it and pulled out the cards, handing them to Claire.

"What kind of snack would you like?" Anne asked.

Claire shuffled through the cards. "Cheese sticks."

"I'll get them," Matt said.

Anne's gaze followed Matt out of the room before she turned back to Claire. "You know that it's your job to get your snack at night? Right?"

Claire nodded. "I'm sorry."

"There's nothing to be sorry about. You're still learning to manage your diabetes. All I ask is that you remember that you're in control, so you take responsibility. Right?"

"Right." Claire gave a soldierly nod of her head.

Matt returned and handed his daughter the cheese sticks.

"I'm sorry I was bad," she murmured as she took them.

Anne reached down to hug the little girl. "Oh, sweetie. Your blood sugar isn't about being good or bad. You are not your diabetes. You are the same wonderful Claire if your glucose levels are high or low."

A wobbly smile appeared.

"This is all about helping you to stay healthy. It's true for all of us. We all want to stay healthy, and I bet your eating choices are helping your father eat healthier, too."

Anne glanced at Matt.

"I hate to admit it, but Anne is right. Claire, you saw my refrigerator when you first moved in. I was eating nothing but junk food. Now I eat healthy like you and I feel better."

"Really?" Claire asked as she bit into her second cheese stick.

"Really." He smiled at her. "We're a team. We're going to do this together."

"Can Anne be on our team?"

"She is right now."

She is right now. Anne mulled the words. Was Matt trying to tell her something? She looked at the small pink clock on Claire's bedside table. "It's getting late."

"Could you stay a few more minutes? Until I fall asleep?" Claire begged.

Anne looked up at Matt and he nodded his approval.

"Okay." She eased into the wicker chair next to the bed. Claire reached out to hold Anne's hand, the other she tucked around her stuffed animal.

"Thank you for coming over," she whispered. Her voice said she was very much still a little girl who needed reassurances that everything would be okay.

Anne leaned down to press a kiss on the top of Claire's silky head. "You're welcome. Your father will check your glucose one more time tonight, and I'm sure everything will be fine. Now go back to sleep and I'll see you on Monday."

Claire nodded and minutes later her soft rhythmic breathing indicated she was asleep.

Anne slid her hand from beneath the smaller one and rose from the chair. She stretched her arms, her eyes upon the girl who slept peacefully.

Matt was very fortunate to have such a wonderful daughter in his life. Out in the living room she found him sitting, staring at his folded hands.

He stood when she entered the room. "I'll walk you out."

"You have a nice little place," she said.

"Emphasis on the little?"

Anne smiled. "Not at all. And it's much tidier than I expected."

He released a small deprecatory chuckle.

"Right. That would be because I straightened it really fast while you were on your way over."

"That wasn't necessary."

"Oh yeah, it was." As he walked past the couch, Matt grabbed a kitchen towel off the cushion. "I'm trying to train Stanley to do housework, but it's been slow going."

"If you can manage that, I'll consider getting a dog. Possibly two."

"The downside is he wants a biscuit every time he does anything."

She grinned and looked around. "Where is he?"

"I let him out in the yard once more for the night."

Matt pushed open the screen and followed her down the short walk to her truck. "Dogs take time, and you were right. You're too busy for a dog. I don't know how you have time for Claire."

"I suppose we make time for things we want to have in our life." She pulled her keys from her pocket.

"Thanks for coming over," he said.

"No problem."

Hands thrust in his pockets, Matt stared hard and long at her for a moment. The planes of his face were stark in the harsh light of the streetlamps.

"No," he finally said. "This isn't like thanks for letting me borrow a cup of sugar. You've done an amazing job with Claire. You've changed both of our lives. Thank you. I mean that."

"I, um…" She floundered, searching for a response.

"No need to say anything. Please, just know that we appreciate you. You're a good friend. Coming over tonight only proves that."

Matt leaned closer until his lips gently kissed her forehead. She stood very still, her eyes momentarily drifting closed, savoring the moment.

When he stepped away, the night air separated the distance between them once more. Anne reached out to unlock the truck.

"Good night, Matt."

"'Night, Anne."

The engine purred and she pointed the vehicle toward home, grateful the streets were empty as she drove slowly while pondering what had just happened.

He was grateful? If only he knew how much he and Claire had changed her life in a few short weeks. She had purpose beyond her job, beyond the roses in her garden and beyond her aunt.

Her black-and-white life was infused with color. The colors of joy, excitement and hope. She touched her forehead where Matt's lips had sweetly awakened something that had been asleep inside her for too long, and realized that she wanted more. Much more, and that more included Matt and Claire.

But she suspected a real life entailed more than just Saturdays. There were so many things demanding her attention right now. How many of those could she juggle before they all fell apart?

What she wanted really didn't matter when she sensed that Matt was moving away from her, not toward. Was there a way to encourage him to take a step of faith and trust her?

Only the Lord could answer that.

Chapter Nine

Late. She'd overslept. *She never overslept.*

Anne toweled her hair dry and slathered on moisturizer. Rubbing the lotion into her face and neck, she dashed to her closet, managing to stub her bare toes on the corner of the bed on the way. Dancing around the room in pain cost her dearly, as another minute she didn't have ticked by.

She yanked a clean pair of scrubs, making the plastic hanger fly and land across the room next to the antique oak armoire. Pants on, drawstring tied. Next, a long, white T-shirt, followed by a scrub top. Name tag in hand, Anne grabbed her purse and keys.

Sadly, there was no time for a go-cup of coffee today.

Her aunt wouldn't be home until tonight. Monday night. That meant one less thing to check on as she headed out the door.

When the traffic light turned red, Anne

clipped back her hair and attached her name tag. Past two more mailboxes, turn left and then approximately fifteen more minutes. Long ago she'd timed the drive from the house to the hospital to ensure she was never late.

Until today.

Ten minutes and thirty seconds later than usual, she pulled into the hospital parking lot, whipped into her supervisor spot and pulled out her makeup bag.

A little mascara and a smear of lip gloss couldn't disguise the dark circles under her eyes, but anything was better than nothing.

Once again sleep had eluded her. There was too much on her mind. Between Matt and Claire, her aunt and the house, she'd found herself unable to find that sweet spot of slumber. Finally, late into the night, she'd fallen asleep reciting her most comforting Bible verses, replaying the moment when Matt's lips had touched her forehead, over and over.

Anne raced through the ER doors as her cell phone began to ring.

Marta stood at the reception desk with surprise all over her face. "I was this close—" she indicted with two fingers "—from calling Sam to check on you."

Anne glanced at her watch. "I'm eleven minutes and forty seconds late. Who calls the sheriff when someone is less than twelve minutes late?"

"You've worked here for ten years. You're *always* a disgustingly and annoyingly fifteen minutes early to work every single day, making the rest of us look like slugs. You rarely take vacation days and never call in sick. Did I mention that you are absolutely, positively, never, ever late?"

"'Cept today," Juanita said with a smirk. She handed Anne a mug filled with coffee. "Black and strong, just the way you like it, boss."

"Thank you." Anne breathed in the rousing aroma.

"What's the occasion?" Juanita asked.

"Occasion?"

"Why you're late. Must be a doozy. I can't wait to hear all the juicy details."

Anne sipped the coffee. "I overslept?" she offered.

"Pshh. Maybe you were dreaming about a tall, blond contractor?" Juanita cocked her head. "Were you dreaming about Mr. Hunky?"

"Maybe I just had insomnia."

"How did it go Saturday?" Marta asked.

"Oh, you know. It was just dinner."

"Yes. I am aware of that, but it was dinner with Matt and Claire," Marta said.

"Dinner with a ten-year-old."

"Come on," Juanita groaned, gesturing with her usual drama. "You're not going to hold out on us, are you? We're trying to live vicariously through you, but I am telling you that so far, your life has been B as in *boring*."

Marta laughed. "I can't believe I'm agreeing with her, however, she does have a point."

"What point was that?"

"We want details," Juanita said. "In fact we demand details. After all, I did provide my share of information about my blind date last month."

"That was an overshare," Marta commented dryly. "You probably should stop now. You are not helping our case here."

Juanita raised her shoulders, her black eyes wide with feigned innocence.

"Did you have a good time at least?" Marta asked.

"What Marta means is did he kiss you?"

Anne's eyes flew open and she swallowed a large swig of coffee and began to cough.

"Oh, come on. You think Heimlich is going to get you out of talking?" Juanita asked. "We want to know all about your date."

"It wasn't a date," she mumbled.

Juanita shoved her hands onto her ample hips. "Hmm, there is something here you aren't telling us. I can smell romance a mile away."

"That's my face lotion."

"You think it is," the unit secretary shot back, "but I know better."

Anne scoffed. "I'm going to do the budget. Hold my calls."

She shut her office door and sniffed the air. She smelled nothing. What was Juanita talking about?

Romance? She only wished it was true. Matt was trying to subtly push her out of his life, which meant that, as usual, there was no romance within miles of her, whether she liked it or not.

The door of the construction office opened and Manny climbed down the steps and pulled off his hard hat. "Matt, Delia just called. She had a phone call from a lady named Williams from Social Services. Are you in trouble?"

"I could be in trouble. I usually am." Matt grinned as he finished tying down a stack of lumber on his flatbed. "However, I have no idea why she would be calling me." He pulled out his cell phone and grimaced. "Looks like I had it on silent. I missed a few calls."

"Delia said to tell you that Mrs. Williams is stopping by tonight to chat with you after she visits Delia to observe Claire's daytime care. You're supposed to call back if her stopping by is problematic." Manny frowned. "Delia got the distinct impression that it better not be problematic."

He shook his head. "What do you think this is all about?"

"You don't know anything about this?"

"Nope."

"The question is…who called Social Services on you. And why?"

"I don't know, but I'm going to find out." Matt hit autodial.

"Who are you calling?"

"Anne."

The phone rang several times before Anne picked up.

"Matt, is Claire okay?"

"Yes. Sorry to bother you. Do you happen to have any idea why a Mrs. Williams from Social Services is contacting me?"

"The hospital was required to contact their offices when your daughter was found on the park bench. I've been sending in weekly updates regarding Claire's progress in her treatment plan."

Treatment plan? All this time he thought Anne was spending time with Claire because she wanted to.

He took a deep breath. "You didn't think about telling me? And here I figured your help with Claire was personal, not because you had to give a report."

Anne released a small gasp. "Matt, you know that I love spending time with Claire." Her voice chilled. "As for Social Services, I apologize, because I thought you were aware. I can assure you that my reports have all been favorable."

"Favorable? What about Claire's hypoglycemic event on Saturday? Will that sound favorable?"

Matt heard her intake of breath before the line went silent. He immediately took a big step back from his anger.

"Okay, I guess I'd better apologize myself before I mess everything up. I'm sorry. That was fear speaking. I know better."

"Matt, your daughter has diabetes. You have done everything you can as a parent to ensure her success as she learns how to maintain her new lifestyle. I'm sure the representative is only calling for a home visit."

"Yeah. She's stopping by tonight. That's not much warning."

"They do that. It's all part of the protocol before they close your file. You'll do absolutely fine."

"Why am I still not so sure?"

"Look, this is all new to you. I understand. But believe me, you're doing a great job and so is Claire."

"Maybe you could prep me for the visit."

"Did I mention that you're going to do fine? This is more about parenting and less about diabetes. The best advice I can give you is to be yourself."

"Why do I not find that reassuring? Being myself is what got me into this situation."

"You're exaggerating. I think you're a very good father."

"I wish I believed that," he said as he ended the call.

"What are you going to do?" Manny asked.

Matt grabbed his car keys. "What do you think I'm going to do? Clean my house."

"You want help?"

"Nah, a little housecleaning will be good to run off my frustration."

He headed to his truck, muttering. As if things hadn't been challenging enough since he'd hit town. Now he was going to be inspected. What if he didn't pass? Would they take Claire away from him because his toilet bowl wasn't sparkling? Or because he didn't serve the right vegetables with dinner? Would this social worker person check his sock drawer, too? What about Stanley? Maybe she wasn't a fan of dogs. Then what? Would he lose his dog, as well?

Lord, You said you wouldn't give me more than I could handle, and I'm pretty much at that point. I need Your help.

"Who was with your daughter when she was found?"

"Stanley."

"Stanley? What's Stanley's last name?"

"Ah, this is Stanley." Matt patted the dog's head. "He's a black Labrador retriever."

The tension in the room was palpable as the large, square, humorless woman looked from

Matt to Stanley. The dog sat quietly on his haunches hoping for a biscuit yet instinctively knowing this was not the time to whine for one. Even the dog was scared of the lady with the huge briefcase who sat across the kitchen table from Matt.

Matt dared to pretend he was scratching his arm while peeking at his watch. An hour. She'd been grilling him for an hour, stopping only to type on her laptop and make distinct noises of displeasure under her breath. Surely she had enough information for her report and several more by now.

She raised her bushy brows and glanced over the top of her glasses at him yet again. Approval was nowhere to be seen. "Generally dogs are not considered substitutes for adult supervision, unless they are registered service dogs."

Matt scrambled for a response.

"Look, Claire recently lost her mother. She and I have… Well, to tell you the truth, I didn't know I had a daughter until a few months ago. This whole parenting thing is new to me. And the diabetes diagnosis was discovered that day. The day she was with Stanley."

The woman paused, considering his words.

"You and your daughter are new to Paradise, aren't you?"

"Yes. I wanted Claire with me. I've already missed nine…ten years of her life."

The woman checked off several boxes on a form and then typed quickly on her laptop. "You'll both need family counseling if I decide to close out your file."

"If?"

"I can't close the file unless I am fully confident that the home situation is in her best interest."

"In her best interest?"

"Mr. Clark—"

"Mr. Clark what? I'm her father."

Silence ensued. He'd apparently crossed the line by verbalizing his frustration.

The woman glanced at her notes. "She has a maternal grandmother in Denver."

"Who is financially and emotionally unable and unwilling to care for her. Claire was living with her pastor's family."

The doorbell rang and Matt jumped to his feet, eager for a diversion before his frustration took over completely and got him into trouble. "Excuse me."

He realized it was Anne behind the screen well before he got to the door. Relief slapped him in the face.

She had obviously come directly from work; she was still in her scrubs. Matt could only offer a prayer that somehow Anne would and could help.

"Anne?"

"I thought you could use a little moral support."

The tension in his shoulders eased as he let her in the house. "You have no idea."

"Oh, I do. I've been on the other side of the table more than once, interviewing family members. I know it's not easy."

"Not easy? That woman is scary."

"Bess is a marshmallow. I've known her for years."

He rubbed his jaw. "Are we talking the same woman?"

"Bess Williams. I admit she comes off as intimidating, but it's all part of the job. She wears emotional armor to get the job done and to protect herself from the grind of the difficult issues she deals with day in and day out. Even a small neighborly community like Paradise has its share of heartbreaking situations involving children."

"I'll have to trust you on that. To be fair to my guest, I guess I never thought of it that way, either."

Anne glanced around. "Where's Claire?"

"Still at Delia's."

"Bess is in the kitchen?"

Matt nodded.

Anne moved confidently past him and straight into the lion's den.

"Anne!" A grin transformed Bess Williams's face. The woman stood and edged her girth around the table to embrace Anne with her meaty arms.

Matt stood stunned at the exchange.

"Sit, Anne. Tell me what you're doing here, dear."

Anne waited until Matt sat and then pulled up a chair next to him.

"Matt is a friend. We've known each other since college. I thought he could use a little support. Life has been a little rough for him lately and I wanted you to know that he's really doing everything he can for Claire."

"That's quite an endorsement." Bess looked at Matt, confusion registering in her eyes behind the thick bifocals. "I've known Anne a long time. She's never done this before. What makes you so special?"

"I, uh, I don't know."

Bess looked him up and down. "Well, if Anne is on your team I think we can schedule family counseling and close out your file."

"Ma'am?"

She slid a business card across the table and closed her laptop. "Call and schedule an appointment. The counselor will send me a report and we'll be done."

"That's all?"

"I can find more, if you like, but I'm confident that if Anne says you're a good parent, you are."

Matt, Anne and Stanley followed Bess to the front door.

"I wish you and your daughter the best, Mr.

Clark. And if I were you, I'd be thanking the good Lord that Anne Matson is your friend."

"Yes, ma'am."

He stood for a moment staring at Bess Williams until she got in her car and disappeared. Then he turned to Anne.

"That was terrifying. It made me really realize how much I want to be a good father to Claire. How much I really love her."

"Oh, Matt."

"Would it be okay to hug you? I feel like I've been given a gift and you made it possible. You and the Lord."

Anne nodded and he wrapped his arms around her, content simply to hold her for a moment. She fit perfectly in his arms, her head tucked beneath his chin. Exactly as he remembered.

Then the moment shifted. She moved away from him, shyly, using one hand to shove her bangs out of her face.

Matt laughed. "You missed some." He reached out to push a wayward strand away from her eyes. His hand lingered, outlining the curve of her ear and then cupping the back of her head as he bent his head to touch his lips to hers.

Her lashes fluttered and finally closed as their lips met.

She tasted like coming home. He would have liked nothing more than to deepen the kiss. But he didn't. Matt judiciously stepped away, his hands returning to his sides.

"I'm sorry, Anne. I guess I got carried away with the moment."

She nodded.

"Thank you. Did I say that already?" he murmured.

She, too, had stepped back, into a safe space, where she took a deep breath, composing herself. The self-sufficient walls were back up again. "You don't have to thank me. We're friends. I care for you and Claire, and I believe in both of you."

"I know," he said. "That's the amazing part of all this."

They glanced at each other.

"We should probably pretend that kiss didn't happen," Matt said.

She jerked back at the words. "Should we?"

"Yeah. Probably so."

Though he'd said the words, he didn't sound very convincing, even to his own ears. Why was it every time he was around her he became confused about what he wanted and where he was going?

She looked at her watch. "I've got to run. The hardware store closes soon."

"Another big hammer project?"

"Sort of." Anne paused and narrowed her eyes.

"I'm ignoring the fact that you insulted my hammer collection for the moment."

Matt smiled. "So what are you working on?"

"One of the second-floor windows is broken. I've got cardboard over it now, but if it rains, I'll be in trouble."

"I do that stuff for a living, you know. Let me fix your window for you."

She shook her head. "That's not necessary."

"Anne, you've done so much for my little family. Let me do what I do well, for you and your aunt. It's not much, but it would make me feel like I'm helping a friend in return."

For a moment she simply stared at him, her big brown eyes conflicted.

"This isn't a commitment. It's a broken window. I'll be by on Saturday. That work for you?"

"Saturday?"

"Yeah. It's sort of becoming our day, isn't it? You and me and Claire." He looked at her. "Friends just hanging out."

"Sure," she agreed, suddenly quiet.

"So, see you then?"

"Okay. I'll have the glass ready."

"Great. But no need to get supplies. I have everything we'll need," he said.

"You have a ladder that reaches the second floor?"

"I do."

"I was going to rent one." Anne pulled her keys from her scrub pants' pocket. "Thank you."

"Are you kidding? This doesn't come close to thanking you for all you've done."

"I could have fixed the window myself. You know that, right?" Her chin was high as she said the words.

"I never doubted it," he said. "You probably have a complete set of socket wrenches, too."

Anne's face lit up. "I do."

Matt only laughed. "You're the only princess I know who fixes her own castle."

She smiled and got into her truck.

As Matt headed to his truck to pick up Claire, the irony of the situation didn't escape him. "I'm helping to repair the house that I am supposed to tear down," he muttered. "And I'm trying desperately not to fall in love with a woman who walked away from me the last time I offered her my heart."

There was something very wrong with the picture. Very wrong and he couldn't shake the sense of foreboding that those thoughts brought with them.

Chapter Ten

"Are you sure you're going to be okay with me coming in late, Marta?" Anne asked into her cell phone.

"Anne, really, we're good. I'm sort of excited that you're coming in late."

"Now you sound like Juanita," Anne muttered.

"Ha! No worries. And remember, we've got those nursing students today, so we have extra staff if we need them."

"I don't know, sometimes having too many untrained hands can be worse than being short-staffed."

"Juanita loves putting them to work. It will be fine."

"Okay, I'm going to leave them to you." She paused. "Thank you. Please say a prayer that I can get in to see the mayor. This is my last shot until the meeting tonight."

"I thought you had an appointment at his office."

"Not exactly. I've tried twice, but his secretary keeps stalling, telling me he'll talk to me before the town hall meeting, which is a terrible idea. He'll be distracted then."

"So, where are you?"

Anne glanced across the street at the town hall building. "I'm sitting in my car right now waiting for someone to show up at his office."

"So your plan is to bluster your way in?"

She shrugged, though she knew Marta couldn't see her frustration. "Basically."

"He lives down the street from me. Goodness, if I had known, we could have stopped by his house. He mows his lawn on Saturday mornings. We could have casually walked by with a big glass of chilled lemonade and some of Patti Jo's cookies. That would have done the trick."

"Casually bribe the mayor?" A laugh burst from her lips. "Is that what you're suggesting?"

"Your aunt would call it being a savvy businesswoman."

Anne laughed again. "I agree. Which is why I already picked up a bag of cookies."

"Smart move, though you know that none of this would be necessary if you'd simply ask Matt about the house. He's building the road, after all, so he must have some insight into why they chose to build it right in the middle of your house."

"I can handle this myself."

"Of course you can. You take care of everything yourself, but it couldn't hurt to ask him."

"We don't have that kind of relationship."

"You see him often enough, thanks to Claire. It seems to me that you don't have to have a relationship to ask him a question."

Anne took a deep breath. "What I'm saying is that he's only the contractor. The town made the decision. I'm only going to see the mayor to see why, and to possibly persuade them to build their road elsewhere." She paused. "Besides, I don't want to get Matt involved in my personal problems. Boundaries are very important."

"I think he's already involved."

Marta's words made her pause. It was as though she could read her mind or at least her intentions.

As though she, too, had heard Matt's words on Saturday. *Sometimes God uses His people to help each other*, he'd said.

"And I believe in boundaries as long as they aren't really fences created by fear," Marta continued.

"Marta."

"Fine, but you know I'm absolutely an I-told-you-so person and eventually I will tell you that I told you so."

"I'm willing to take the risk," Anne said.

"What's going on with the National Registry?"

"I spent hours filling out the forms online. My

eyeballs were rotating independently by the time I was done. But that whole process still isn't a given, either."

"I don't understand. Why not?"

"Technically, the house may qualify due to the architectural significance. The first step was to nominate the property and submit all the forms. Which of course, I did. The second step is the Review Board. Their meeting is at the Colorado History Center in Denver in three months. Three months from now is not going to help my problem. And historic registration approval doesn't guarantee the house won't be torn down if the Town of Paradise eminent domain overrules."

"You certainly have done your research."

"Trust me. If there was a possible way to save the house, I've researched it in the past two weeks."

"Oh, my goodness. I'm so sorry. This must be extremely difficult for you. Not knowing if you have to move out of your house by the deadline." Marta sighed. "Have you thought about taking some time off to sort this all out?"

"No. Work is the only normal thing in my life."

"Anne, that's a sad commentary. You work in an emergency department."

"It is what it is."

"What does your aunt say?"

"Are you kidding? I'm not telling Aunt Lily until moving day, if it comes to that."

A car door slammed and Anne swiveled around in her seat. "Oh, I've got to go. He beat his secretary into work today. Now's my chance."

She slipped the phone into her purse and pulled the strap over her shoulder. Careful not to close her truck door too loudly, Anne crossed Main Street and followed the mayor.

As his key slid into the building's door lock, Anne cleared her throat.

J. D. Rutherford whirled around, his eyes wide. "Anne, you scared me."

"Sorry, J.D."

He eyed her navy scrubs as he pushed open the big, glass doors. "On your way to work?"

"Yes, sir. But I was hoping for a minute of your time first."

He swallowed. Did she imagine the nervous twitch of his left eye? "Most folks schedule with my secretary. She can get you on my calendar."

"I tried that, but I keep getting the runaround and I'm nearly out of time. The town hall meeting is tonight."

Anne looked around the small office. "Where is your secretary anyhow?"

"Vacation day. But she'll be at the meeting later."

J.D. adjusted the collar of his starched, white dress shirt and ran a hand over his abdomen where the buttons barely contained his girth. He glanced at his watch. "I have about five minutes before my first meeting of the day."

"Thank you, sir."

"Coffee? The pot was set to auto brew. Should be done." He nodded toward a counter in the waiting area.

"I've had my quota, thank you." She handed him a white pastry bag.

"What's this?" he asked, brows raised.

"Cinnamon raisin oatmeal. Your favorite, as I recall."

He faltered for a moment and then smiled. "Why, thank you. You always were a favorite of mine, Anne."

She smiled.

"Come on in to the office and have a seat," he said.

She eased down onto the worn, caramel-colored leather sofa across from his oak desk and glanced around. "It still looks the same as it did when I was little."

"Your aunt was in and out of here more times than I can count back then. Now, there was a steamroller." He chuckled.

She pinned him with her gaze. "I'm not here to steamroll you, J.D., but I would like some answers."

"Anne, I'll do my best, but you may not want

to hear what I have to say." His leather chair creaked as he settled into it.

She released a breath of air and nodded, knowing all too well he was probably right.

"Frankly, I'm a bit surprised you didn't contact me when the first letter came out. What took you so long?"

"I didn't get the first or second letter." She clasped her hands. "My aunt may have hidden them. Lately her mental status has been deteriorating."

He shook his head slowly. "I'm sorry to hear that. You know how much I respect and admire Lily."

"Thank you." Anne bit her lip. "Why my house, J.D.?"

"I admit that when I saw the plans, at first I was alarmed on a personal level. I've been friends with your family since I was a boy." He picked up a silver pen from his desk and frowned before he met her gaze. "But the good citizens of Paradise pay me to put their needs as a whole before my personal feelings. It's my fiduciary duty."

"I understand that, but surely there's another way to route traffic to the lake."

"We've got mountains in the way. This is the most cost-effective plan and it's a mighty good one. Why it even allows for future widening of the road if the town grows enough to warrant that."

"I'm not convinced that the road couldn't come up from behind the lake."

"That routes traffic nearly two miles out of the way. Besides, the spring run-off is on that side of the mountain. You know yourself how many times that road is closed due to landslides."

"I think a clever developer could have come up with a solution."

"Then probably you should be talking to the developers."

"Who's that?"

"Matthew Clark and Manuel Seville. First Construction. I thought you knew that."

Matt. Her heart began to race. Had she known deep down inside that this would all come full circle back to Matt?

"Anne, are you all right?"

She stood and turned toward the door. "Thank you for your time."

"You know you have the right to make your appeal at the town hall meeting tonight. Present an option that the board can approve. We'd like nothing better."

"You said yourself there is no other option."

This time it was the mayor who released a frustrated breath in response. "You never know."

No, you never did know. Anne pushed open

the door and stood outside on the sidewalk, the cool morning air wrapping itself around her.

First Construction had created and submitted the plans that would destroy her home. She should have realized it, but maybe she really didn't want to know the truth.

And she didn't want Matt to be the bad guy in all this.

Apparently she'd been fooling herself.

Marta knocked gently and stepped into Anne's office. "How'd it go with the mayor?"

"Don't ask."

"That good, huh?"

Anne shook her head.

"Do you want me to go with you to the town hall meeting tonight?"

"I'll go, too," Juanita commented, peeking her dark head into the room.

"Hmm?" Anne looked up from the book on her desk and blinked.

"Honey, are you okay?" Juanita said. She straightened and walked up to Anne's desk. "You've been awfully distracted the past few days."

Distracted? Yes, maybe she was. The mental footage of Matt's kiss was enough to keep her distracted and add to her confusion.

Pretend it didn't happen, he'd said. Right. Pretend it didn't happen while she was also pretending he wasn't responsible for the plans to destroy her home. Now she knew why he'd said that.

"Anne?" Marta repeated. "The meeting?"

"Sorry, I was reading the state laws on eminent domain."

"Eminent domain?" Juanita asked. "Okay, I give up. What is that?"

"It basically means that the town can do whatever it wants for the good of the town."

"What about the meeting?" Marta persisted.

Anne stood and began to clear her desk. "No need. I can—"

"We know," Marta interrupted, her tone as droll as ever. "You can handle it yourself. That wasn't the question. Do you want us to go with you?"

Anne's shoulders sagged as she released the weight of taking on the burden alone. "Yes. Yes, I do. Thank you." She sank back down into her desk chair. "What am I going to do if I lose the house?"

"We need to pray," Juanita said. She hustled into the room and kicked the door shut with her foot.

"Not here," Anne said.

"Yes. Here," Juanita said sharply.

Marta closed the blinds on the window that faced the hallway, and they both took Anne's hands in theirs.

"Lord, we turn this situation over to You and

ask You for wisdom as we go into the meeting. We pray Your will is done. Amen."

"Thanks, Juanita," Anne said.

"Honey, that's what friends are for. We hold each other's arms up when the other is burdened. We're Aaron to your Moses. We shall prevail."

Anne could only smile at Juanita's enthusiasm. "I don't think I'm any Moses, but I appreciate the sentiment and both of you."

"Now let's discuss coordinating our outfits for tonight," Juanita said as she plopped onto the corner of Anne's desk.

Marta began to laugh. "We're wearing coordinating outfits?"

"Yes. That's what sisters do," Juanita said. "And we're sisters in the Lord, aren't we?"

Marta doubled over, laughing.

"I don't know what you think is so funny. This is serious business," Juanita said.

"I want to know what we're wearing," Marta said. "The visual I'm getting of the three of us dressed like triplets in one of your crazy ensembles with matching hats isn't going away anytime soon."

"I'll have you know I am considered a fashion diva where I come from," Juanita countered.

Anne leaned back in her chair and grinned as the two continued their repartee. She was so grateful for these two women.

* * *

All eyes were on Anne as she walked into the meeting room at town hall.

"Ooh, ooh, we should have brought Patti Jo's cinnamon rolls. This group could use some sweetening up," Juanita muttered as she followed Anne. "What a bunch of sour faces." She shivered.

"They have coffee," Marta said with a glance at the giant coffee urn at the back of the room. "Come on, Juanita, you can help me. We'll scout things out."

Anne sat in a chair near the back of room. A moment later her closest neighbor, Mabel Hotchkins, sat down next to her.

"Hello, Mrs. Hotchkins."

The woman nodded, though she didn't crack a smile on her pasty face. "I understand you're the only holdout."

Anne jerked back in surprise. "Excuse me? I thought that information was confidential," Anne said.

"This is Paradise."

That was certainly true enough. And hadn't she said the same thing herself recently. Sometimes living in a small town was as big a curse as it was a blessing.

"You know," Mabel continued, "the town is offering a generous amount for the houses. In fact it's enough to allow my husband and me to move down to Alamosa to be near our grandchildren."

"You want me to sell my house so you can be near your grandchildren?"

"I want you to think of the big picture. There are three houses. You aren't the only one. Hannah Oster and her sister Sadie can't be here tonight. Sadie is in Denver for some specialized cardiac surgery. Selling that house expeditiously means they can buy a little place with less maintenance and pay off their medical bills."

The arrow hit its mark and Anne folded her arms protectively across her chest, shielding herself from further pain. "Mrs. Hotchkins…"

"You call me Mabel. I've known your family since they first came to the valley. Known you since you were this big." Mabel gestured with her hand.

Anne took a deep breath. "Mabel, thank you for the update. I imagine that since you know my family so well, you're also aware of how long my aunt's home has been here in Paradise. Well over one hundred years. In fact, that house is all that my aunt and I have left of our family."

"Family isn't about houses." Mabel tapped her heart with her palm twice. "It's about what's in here."

"Pardon me," Juanita said from where she stood in the aisle.

Both Anne and Mabel looked up.

Juanita narrowed her eyes and thrust out her chin. "You're in my seat."

"I was just leaving." Mabel stood and backed out of the row.

"Was that woman harassing you?" Juanita handed Anne a foam cup of coffee.

"No, merely a bit of a guilt trip. It worked. Now I feel absolutely awful."

"Stop that," Marta interjected as she sat on the other side of Anne. "It's your house. You are entitled to save it, despite what anyone else thinks."

The room began to slowly fill up as homeowners and local businessmen and -women wandered in, their chatter creating a low buzz as they greeted each other.

When the mayor's secretary entered, an agenda was passed out.

"Uh-oh. *Robert's Rules*," Marta whispered.

"Why 'uh-oh'?" Anne asked.

"No starting time for each issue. The easiest way to defeat an issue is to take up so much meeting time that the issue you want to squash never comes up. They may try to keep you from having an opportunity to speak."

"These are my friends, my neighbors. Why would they do that to me?"

"Anne, get real. When it comes to love and money, the chaff is burned away with the wheat."

Anne turned to Juanita. "I think you messed up that verse. What exactly are you trying to say?"

"What she's trying to say in Juanita-speak is that this is when you find out who your friends really are."

"I still don't understand," Anne said.

"Honey," Juanita said, "I was talking to folks while I was getting coffee. Apparently if you don't sign the contract by the due date, then your house will stall the project. That means the town will lose money. The contractor will lose money. And if that road isn't built, then the businesses of this town will not reap the rewards, which would have translated to increased tourism. That means businesses will lose money."

Anne sat very still, absorbing Juanita's words. Not signing was going to hurt the town. The words spun 'round and 'round, tightening like a noose. Her only defense was that she had only just received the letter. She hadn't had time to consider the whole picture.

"It doesn't matter," she said aloud.

"What?" Marta asked.

She turned to look at her friends. "It doesn't matter that I just got the letter. From the moment I received it, I've only been thinking about me and Lily. What this means to us. I've been so selfish."

"Don't be so hard on yourself," Marta said. "Your response is perfectly normal. I'd feel the same way."

"Maybe the Lord doesn't want to save my house," Anne said.

"Our maybes don't matter. We didn't pray for your will to be done," Juanita said. "We prayed for His will to be done. And it will be. We're just standing in faith now. Waiting on Him."

"Tell that to the people in this room."

"How long do you have until the contract has to be signed?" Marta asked.

"The end of the month, which is coming right up."

The mayor's secretary tapped the microphone. "Please be seated. We'll be reading and approving the minutes of our last meeting."

Anne didn't hear the words; instead she glanced around the room. There were seventeen hundred people in Paradise and those who were members of the town's small business group were all present.

Patti Jo who owned the bakery and café was here, as was fire chief Jake MacLaughlin, who owned the hardware store, and his wife, Maggie. Several of the local ranchers, the Gallaghers, the Elliotts, and others were in the audience of the small town hall building. Physicians and nurses from the hospital filled the seats, as well. In fact, the room was completely packed and there were people elbow-to-elbow clear into the foyer. Standing against the far wall were Matt and Manny.

Matt nodded to her and she turned her head away in shame.

The gavel rang out and Mayor J. D. Rutherford presided over the meeting.

First the reports of the town officers, boards and standing committees were read, along with the treasurer's report. Anne sat in silent agony, checking her watch often, her eyes on the cold coffee cup in her hand. Everything around her became white noise as she waited.

Finally the report of the special committee dealing with the Paradise Lake Project began. Though her aunt was not named as the remaining homeowner who hadn't yet signed the purchase agreement that would allow the project to proceed, all eyes were on Anne, making it completely obvious everyone knew. Once the deadline arrived, the town had five business days left to decide if they would consider moving forward with action against the remaining homeowner.

"*Consider.* That's the word they used. So don't get yourself all worked up," Marta whispered.

Too late, she was already worked up.

As murmuring began in the audience, Anne slunk lower in her chair.

Finally, as though he couldn't put it off any longer, the mayor tapped the microphone. "Are there any questions?"

Mabel Hotchkins stood and hurried to the microphone in the aisle. "Yes, Mr. Mayor. I want to know if the town is going to file an injunction to force Lily Gray and her great-niece to sign their house over to the town. I believe this action would be for the good of Paradise."

"We've already covered that, Mrs. Hotchkins," J.D. returned. But it was too late. The audience was stirred up, which was clearly what Mabel wanted.

Voices in the room rumbled, getting louder and louder. Some stood and they began to argue. The mayor tapped the microphone with force as he struggled to rein in the meeting.

Anne stood. She stepped over Juanita and pushed through to the aisle and to the closest microphone.

She tapped harder and harder until the sound of her hand hitting the mike drowned out the voices.

Finally the room was silent.

"You've all had your say. I'd like a chance to share mine." She glanced around, summing up a courage she didn't feel.

If she could manage an emergency department she could do this. Right.

Lord help me.

"I want my friends and neighbors to know that my great-aunt, Lily Gray, and I love Paradise. We also love our home. We're being asked to choose between two things that have been near and dear to us our entire lives. It's not my intention to do anything that would hurt this town or to stand in the way of what Paradise needs."

Anne took a deep breath. "I'm asking you to allow us a little time to prepare ourselves to do the right thing, whatever that may be."

Ducking her head, she turned around and moved out of the noisy, stuffy room through the meeting room double doors and outside.

"Anne, I'm sorry."

When she turned, Matt was behind her on the sidewalk.

"Matt, I don't understand any of this. I've been like an ostrich with my head in the ground. I'll be hurting Paradise if I don't sign, isn't that right?"

"I can't answer that."

"Well, I'll be hurting your business by stalling the project. Even my friends had the guts to tell me that."

He shoved his hands into his pockets and didn't look at her.

"Why did the road have to be there? Whose idea was that? Yours or Manny's? Couldn't it have gone on the other side of the woods? Why can't I have my house and you have your road somewhere else?"

"Whoa." He held up a hand against the torrent of her questions. "The plans as they are include the best use of the land and the town's money and take into consideration future growth of Paradise. The decision was made without bias."

"I'm sure you're right." She hung her head. "I'm making this all about me. I've only had a short time to think about everything and I guess I just kept hoping that there would be some sort of Godly rabbit-out-of-the-hat solution."

"Anne, look at me."

She raised her head and met his blue eyes. What she saw there worried her.

"The plans for the road?"

"Yes?"

"They were my design. I'm responsible. Not Manny. Only me."

Another arrow to her heart. She stood very still, trying to compose herself.

"You and only you designed the plans that included tearing down my house?"

"I didn't know it was your house when the plans were proposed."

"How could you not know?"

"I'd never been to your home. Think about it. You always kept me away. Once I submitted the designs it was all out of my hands until the town voted and approved the project. Another contractor would have likely provided a similar solution."

"Why didn't you say something? All these weeks with Claire? Why didn't you tell me?"

He shook his head. "Because deep down inside, I was hoping a solution would present itself, just like you were."

"Are you sure this isn't some sort of retribution for what happened ten years ago?"

Matt's head jerked back just as if he'd been punched. Pain registered on his face and immediately contrition hit her. "Do you really believe that?" he rasped.

"I don't know what I believe anymore." She turned away. "I've got a lot to think about. To pray about."

"Do you want a ride home? Maybe you shouldn't be driving when you're so upset."

"No, I'll be fine."

"Anne, wait."

She faced him once more.

"Do you know why there was so much discussion going on in there after Mabel got up to talk?"

"I thought it was because everyone was angry. Mad at me."

"No. Half the town is on your side. It's your house and they don't agree that the town has the right to take away your home and your land. The Gallaghers and the Elliotts are your biggest supporters. All the ranchers in the valley are. After all, if the town can take your home, they're worried it might also decide to take their land for the betterment of Paradise."

He raised both hands this time, as though trying one last time to reach out to her. "I'm on your side, too, you know. I'm your friend, and friends are there for each other no matter what."

Anne cocked her head. "Funny but someone just said similar words to me before the meeting."

"They were right."

"Yes. Unfortunately we're both in an awkward position."

"Yeah, we are, and I'd do anything to turn back the clock."

"Turn back the clock. I doubt that's the answer for us, Matt."

"So what is the solution?"

"I don't know. No matter what we do, we don't seem to ever get it right."

"Anne, that's so wrong. I don't believe that at all."

She shrugged.

"Deep down inside don't you think that maybe we deserve a second chance? A chance to forget the past and move toward…I don't know, something more?" he asked.

"No." Her heart clutched as she said the words. "You represent possibly the biggest mistake of my life."

"I'm a mistake?" he asked, hurt etched on his face.

She shook her head. "That's not what I mean. I'm telling you that I'm angry at myself for what I did to you. Angry that I didn't fight for us. I'm ashamed of myself, but I can't take back the past.

I can't make it up to you." She inhaled and slowly released the breath.

"You have no reason to trust me, and my mistake will always stand between us."

"You're so wrong and someday I'm going to make you understand."

"Before or after you tear down my house?"

"Anne, that wasn't fair."

"Well, I'm not feeling very fair right now."

The silence that filled the space between them grew larger with each passing second.

"What about tomorrow?" Matt murmured.

"Tomorrow?"

"Your house. The window?"

"Could we postpone that? I think I need some alone time. Can you explain to Claire?"

"I will. But I want you to know that I'm not your enemy. I'm trying to understand how you feel, except, I guess I've never faced losing anything that mattered to me. Except you."

Her gaze flew to his and her heart stumbled at the honesty of his words.

"But I do know that when you're hurting it isn't the time to shut out the people who care for you," he continued.

"Are you telling me that you care for me, Matt?" After all she'd just said, his words both saddened and encouraged her.

"Both Claire and I care for you. We need you. Probably more than you know." He offered a slow, almost wistful smile that said that he wasn't at all surprised that she didn't realize the truth of his words.

"I don't understand how you can forgive me," Anne said.

"I hadn't planned to. Not really." He chuckled. "In fact, my plan included resentment, bitterness and a few other things. But, fortunately, the Lord got a hold of me."

"You're a good man, Matt."

"Don't put me on a pedestal. I've made plenty of mistakes and will probably continue to. All I'm saying is don't turn your back on us. We want to help. We do care."

"You're right. I'll try to remember that."

"Anne, was that the doorbell?"

"I'll get it, Aunt Lily."

"Manny?" Anne grinned when she saw him standing behind the screen with an effervescent smile on his face. The same Manny she remembered. "What are you doing here?"

"I thought it was about time we had a chance to catch up."

"How are you feeling? I'm sorry our paths didn't cross in the hospital. Although, I did see you in the ER."

"So I heard. I don't exactly remember much about that."

She pushed open the screen. "Come in. Come in. How are you feeling?"

"Feeling good and the ribs are healing."

"Then I'd better not give you a bear hug," she said with a smile.

"Who is it, Anne?"

Anne motioned for Manny to follow her to the living room.

"Aunt Lily, this is a friend of mine from college. Manuel Seville."

"Oh, how nice to meet you." Lily stood and carefully maneuvered around her chair with one hand on the furniture at all times. As usual, the lady of the house was dressed for company. Since it was Sunday afternoon she wore a burgundy-print silk shirtdress that set off her white hair. "Did you attend Washington State?"

"No, ma'am. I met your great-niece at the University of Denver."

"Oh. Did she attend?" A deep frown settled on her face. "I can be forgetful these days." She shook her head and shrugged. "Well, no matter. It is certainly a pleasure to meet you."

"The pleasure is all mine, ma'am."

"Aunt Lily, we're going into the kitchen."

"All right, dear. Do serve your friend some of that lemonade. Oh, and be sure to show him the roses."

"I will." She led Manny down the hall to the

oversize kitchen and stood next to the huge oak table. "I heard you got married and have a new baby. Congratulations."

"Thank you." Manny reached for his back pocket. "I said I'd never do this. But I pull out my wallet more in one day than my father ever did."

Anne laughed as she took the billfold from him. "And you should. You have a beautiful family." A pang of longing struck her as she flipped through the pictures. What would it be like to have a family of her very own? For a brief moment her thoughts flew to Matt.

She handed him back his photos and he glanced around at the ceiling moldings and the gingerbread trim at the windows.

"Wow, this place is as amazing as Matt said it was."

"Thank you."

"Big house for two people."

"I suppose my great-great-grandfather had high hopes of filling it up with children, but progeny was never my family's strong suit. Working too much was."

"It's not too late to change that, is it?"

She smiled. "Things don't look hopeful at the moment. I'm not married and the town of Paradise is about to raze the house. The potential for children sliding down the front banister or playing hide-and-seek in the attic is decreasing each day."

"I can see why you want to save the place." He examined the punched-tin ceiling. "You applied for historic registry?"

"Yes. But I won't know for ninety days."

"Why did you wait so long?"

"My aunt hides mail."

Manny blinked. "Excuse me?"

"My aunt hid the mail. I didn't find out about this until two weeks ago."

"Did you tell anyone that?"

"The mayor is aware, but at this point it's out of my hands. And, really, I'm trying to think about the greater good here. I'm simply waiting on the Lord for the next step. I imagine I'll be signing the contract as soon as I get up the energy and courage to drive into town."

"It's a shame. I have to tell you that I hope the Lord comes through, because destroying this house is not something I want to do."

"I appreciate that."

"Original cement-tile floors?" he asked.

Anne nodded. "Yes. The company that did them was apparently well-known for installing all the geometric floors during the time the house was built."

Manny grinned. "I can't believe you know that."

"I read a lot. You should see my stack of library books." She smiled. "May I offer you some of my grandmother's lemonade?"

"No, thanks, I'm fine. But I would like to see those roses."

"Certainly, and we can pick some for your wife."

"She'd love that."

"Let me show you the yard. We have quite the view."

"So I've heard."

Anne opened the French doors and they stepped outside. The fragrance of roses was heavy in the summer air.

Manny didn't wait for an invitation, instead he walked straight to the rose garden. She grabbed a cutting basket and shears and followed slowly behind as he walked down the paver path examining the many varieties.

"I don't know what I like best, the outside architecture, the inside details or this yard."

She could only smile at his appreciative words.

"It would be flat wrong to destroy this house," he finally said, his words firm with purpose. "Flat wrong."

"So you understand my dilemma."

"I do now."

"You haven't told me why you're here, Manny."

"I came by to tell you that Matt didn't know anything about your house when we started this project."

Anne sighed. "He told me that."

"But you have to know that if you don't sign, every day the project is delayed by the road issue we'll be losing money. However Matt will never push you to sign, because he wants to do what's right."

"What is right?"

"I guess only God knows that. But he's single-handedly holding off the town from filing the injunction to force you to vacate."

"Thank you for telling me."

"Anne, is there any chance that you and Matt…"

"We're tentatively friends. That's a good place to be."

"'Tentatively'?"

"Some days are better than others. Lately? Not so good. Things have been challenging."

"He still cares for you."

"I care for him, as well. He's an honorable man. What I did to him ten years ago was unforgivable. While he says he has forgiven me, I can't help but fear that our past has ruined the possibility for a future."

"I think you're wrong."

"That could very well be. I've been wrong about a lot of things lately."

Manny gave her a wry smile. "No, you don't get it. Matt still loves you. I think he's having a hard time admitting it, because he's afraid of getting hurt. But one encouraging word from you…"

"I'm not sure I can offer an encouraging word right now."

"Okay, but do me a favor and add Matt to your prayer list. Maybe the Lord has something to say about him, as well."

"I will. Though truthfully, Manny, I feel like all I'm doing is praying and waiting on the Lord lately. I certainly hope He plans to answer soon."

"A good many prayers are answered in the eleventh hour," he said.

Anne smiled. "God of the eleventh hour. Yes, you're right. I'm going to hold on to those words. Thank you."

Chapter Eleven

"Matt, wait," Manny called.

Shoving a yellow hard hat on his head Matt turned toward his partner. They stood shoulder to shoulder on the gravel drive, right outside the construction office trailer.

"Were you headed out?" Manny asked.

"Yeah. Going to check on the foundations for those condos." He glanced at his watch. "Should start pouring in about an hour. What did you need?"

"I was wondering if you've talked to Anne since the town hall meeting."

Matt shook his head no. "Rough meeting, wasn't it?"

Manny nodded.

"I've tried to stay out of her way. She pretty much accused me of plotting revenge by targeting her house. We canceled Claire's visit with her last weekend. Anne said she needed some alone time."

"You should always be worried when a woman says that."

"What can I do?"

"The question is what are you going to do?"

"Give her the space she asked for. It's been almost a week. I'll see if it's okay to bring Claire by on Saturday, but in general I think I'm just going to fly as far as I can under her radar."

"She doesn't really believe you planned this, you know, and I doubt she really wants you to leave her alone."

"Then why would she say that?"

"Because she was hurting."

"That doesn't make any sense."

"You sure have a lot to learn about women, don't you, pal? When they walk away is the exact time that they want you to go after them."

Matt inched his hard hat to the back of his head with a finger. "Nah. Who told you that?"

"That's just the way it is." Manny shook his head. "I went and talked to her."

"You talked to Anne. When?"

"Last Sunday."

"You're saying I should have gone to her house?" Matt grimaced.

"Probably."

"What could I have done? I've looked at things

from every angle and I don't see that there is any solution."

"Everything can be fixed, Matt. That's what we do for a living."

"We work with the tangible. Last time I checked, mending broken hearts wasn't our specialty."

Manny frowned. "Whose heart is it we're talking about here? Yours or hers?"

"I'm talking about Anne. Her heart is completely broken over that house. I can't say that I blame her, either. The more time I spend in that old Victorian, the more I realize how special it really is."

"I have to agree. I never thought I'd say it, but now I've seen the place."

"Then you agree that it seems almost sacrilegious to destroy a house like that. Especially in our line of work. We're both architects by degree and general contractors by trade. Demolishing something that was meant to stand forever, something as beautiful and solid as that house, is plain wrong"

"Those are my thoughts exactly. There has to be another answer. We just have to dig deeper."

"When you find it, let me know. I've spent hours thinking about this." Matt shook his head. "At any rate, one thing is clear. You were right. If I had talked to her ahead of time I might have at least cushioned the blow somehow."

"We work well together because I'm not a told-you-so guy." Manny offered a smile. "No matter what happens, Anne's got a lot of painful decisions to make. She lost a lot of time because of her aunt. Then there's the fact that the town expects her out, one way or another, in thirty business days from tomorrow."

Matt frowned. "What do you mean she lost a lot of time because of her aunt?"

"Anne never received the first two letters with the town's offer. Only the final notice because it was sent by certified mail. She's certain her aunt hid the other letters."

"Lily?" Matt exhaled in a whoosh. "I didn't know that. Poor Anne. Then this all really is a shock for her. How did you find out so much in one visit?"

"I live with a woman. I've learned to listen very carefully, not only for what they say, but more importantly, for what they don't say."

"Apparently, I don't have your talent. I've made a real mess of things." Matt scraped a hand over his face. "You know, once things get settled here and this project is on autopilot, I'm thinking the best thing for me is to move on."

Manny's jaw slackened as he stared at Matt. "Move on? What do you mean move on?"

"I'm talking about heading back to Denver."

"Denver? Are you serious?"

"As serious as I've ever been."

"I'm your partner. You weren't going to talk to me about it?"

"I'm talking now."

"What about the company?" Manny asked. "We started this thing from the ground up with the two of us. Unless you feel God's leading you somewhere else, why mess with what we have?"

"I haven't decided anything yet. Just tossing some ideas around."

"Maybe I shouldn't ask, but what did you have in mind?"

"I can be here to help you launch projects that come up in the valley, then go back to Denver and work on smaller ones with a pared-down crew. Diversify the company."

"Yeah, and that would work if we had enough cash flow to support two crews. But we don't. We're living paycheck to paycheck until this project is completed." Manny shrugged, looking none too enthused about the idea anyhow. "I don't have to remind you that every cent we have is invested in what we're doing here in Paradise. If we get the lake project we have a good shot at the hospital. But it's going to take the two of us."

"I said I was only thinking about it."

"Yeah, well, I wish you'd think about something else. You're making me nervous. And you don't want to make the guy who handles the finances anxious." He huffed a long breath. "Besides, I thought you and Claire were getting settled in Paradise. She seems pretty happy here, too. School's going to start soon. Delia said she's met some kids her age already."

"I can't settle down in Paradise when I know I've destroyed Anne's life. This town is too small and the more time I spend here the smaller it gets. Constantly running into her would be all kinds of awkward."

"You mean because of the way you feel about her?"

Matt jerked back and looked at Manny. "What? You have X-ray vision now, too?"

"Come on. I've known you for the better part of my life. You wear your heart on your sleeve. Doesn't take Dr. Phil to figure you out."

"Okay, fine. Yeah, that has a lot to do with it. I don't want her to feel like she's obligated to me or my daughter, either."

"Are you sure she feels that way? Seems to me that you're considering some big changes based on a lot of assumptions."

"Am I? I'm not so sure. I've made overtures, feeling her out about forgetting the past and starting over, but I can't help but feel…"

"What?"

"Part of me thinks she really does believe her aunt's predictions about me."

"Cut it out. You're a successful contractor."

"Yeah. Who's living paycheck to paycheck, you just said."

"Look, you need to have a heart-to-heart with Anne before you do anything that you'll regret for another ten years."

Matt stared at his friend and shook his head. "You sure have a lot of answers in your back pocket today, don't you?"

Manny laughed, easing the tension between them. "It only seems that way to you because I can look at the situation objectively. I'd say you're letting your emotions get the better of you. Whatever happened to walking by faith?"

Matt held up his hands. "Whoa. Okay, I know when to quit. We can finish this discussion later. I have to get going."

Manny's only response was to grin.

"Can you keep an eye on Claire until I get done? She's reading in the trailer. I've got a couple more hours here and then she and I will head home early."

"Sure. No problem. I'm going to catch up on some paperwork." His boots echoed on the wood as he pounded up the stairs to the trailer platform. The door of their makeshift office closed with a bang behind him.

Matt shut the tailgate of the truck and reached into his pocket for his keys. A moment later Manny was out on the platform again.

"Hey, Matt. I thought you said Claire was in here," he called out from the doorway.

"She is."

"Not that I can see. And where's Stanley?"

Matt rushed up the stairs and followed Manny inside, his gaze searching every corner. "She was here. Reading."

"Where would she go?" Manny asked.

Matt tossed his hard hat on the desk and paced back and forth in the small space. "She overheard us."

"You think so?"

"Sure. Those side windows are open, and if she heard me talking about moving back to Denver, she probably took off out the back door. Claire's gotten pretty fond of Anne and Lily." Matt shook his head. "I can't believe I was so careless."

"Does she know the shortcut through the woods?"

"Sure she does. So does Stanley."

"That's one smart kid you have, Matt."

"A smart dog, too, thankfully."

He opened the locker where Claire stored her belongings when she came to work with him. Empty. "It looks like she took her diabetic supplies, as well. Her pink backpack is gone."

"Thank the Lord for that," Manny said. "You want me to go with you to Anne's?"

"No, but thanks." Matt gave a quick, dismissive shake of his head. "This will require some one-on-one time with Claire. First, I've got to figure out how I'm going to explain everything that's going on to a ten-year-old. She won't care about anything except why I'm talking about messing with her world again."

"Oh, for goodness' sake, Anne. Go home, would you?"

Anne barely raised her chin from her hand, which was in turn propped up by her arm, to see Marta standing in the doorway of her office. "It's only three in the afternoon on a Thursday."

"You haven't slept in days and you look like you're going to keel over any minute now."

"That good, huh?"

"Yeah, and you know what we'd do if that happens, right?" Juanita appeared in the doorway.

"If you're trying to scare me by threatening to admit me to my own emergency department, it's working."

"Good," Juanita continued.

"I checked with HR," Marta said. "While they wouldn't reveal the exact numbers due to some sort of privacy ridiculousness, they assured me you have enough sick and vacation days to take off the rest of the week without even touching this year's accrual."

"You did not."

Marta laughed. "No, but it remains true."

Anne reached for her purse. "You know what? I am going to go home, and I'll be back and punctual come Monday. I need to stop by the library to pick up some books. Plus, this will give me plenty of time to schedule an appointment to sign the contract and then decide what I'm going to do next. After all, I have to pack and find a place to live, as well."

"As usual, you're an overachiever. That's a pretty ambitious list for four days," Marta said. "And all by yourself, as well."

"It's a start. You taking off a few days is huge." Juanita patted Anne's arm. "I'm proud of you, sweetie."

"She's right, and I'm proud, as well. When you get things sorted out let us know and we'll have a packing party," Marta said.

"A packing party?" Anne repeated.

"Sure. You invite everyone you know. All you have to do is feed them. The packing gets done in one day."

"I'm not sure that's a practical idea. I can handle most of it myself anyhow."

"Yes." Marta released a sigh. "We know. You can do everything. But it's more fun with your friends."

"Besides," Juanita said, "you have no idea what you're dealing with here. You've lived in that house almost thirty years. Your aunt's been in it for another forty-five. That's a good seventy-five years of accumulation." She snorted and shook her head. "Sounds like more than even you can tackle, super girl."

"She's right. On second thought, just rent a Dumpster."

Anne laughed. "You know, I'm starting to feel better just talking to you two. Maybe I'll go ahead and stay until five."

"No!" The word burst from Marta's and Juanita's lips at the same time. Then they began to laugh as they took position on either side of her and led her out of her office and down the hall toward the emergency room doors.

"Go home," Juanita said. "You've got a major life crisis going on and you need to be there, not at work. I can pull out that life-changes stress test and prove it to you, if you want."

"She's right. You aren't eating. You can't sleep. In fact, maybe it would be better if I call the sheriff to drive you," Marta commented.

"I'll be fine, ladies." The doors of the emergency department swooshed open and Anne headed to the parking lot, leaving her friends smiling.

Would she be okay? Anne didn't know, but by the time her truck pulled into her driveway she'd admitted the truth to herself. It was time to make some hard decisions.

Anne just sat for a while. For once, she couldn't bear to look at the house. She'd let the stately lady down.

When she did look up, it was to see Stanley

wantonly bounding around from the backyard, his leash flapping in the air.

"Stanley?"

She opened her door and got out. The dog danced in enthusiastic circles around her.

A moment later Claire rounded the corner, her face and sweatshirt speckled with mud and her sneakers and jeans wet.

"Claire, what are you doing here? What happened to you?"

The round face was resolute. "I ran away."

"What do you mean? Your house is over five miles in the other direction. How did you get here?"

"I was at the construction office. Sometimes I get to spend the day there helping. It's on the other side of the woods. Stanley came with me."

"You ran away and played in the mud?"

A small smile appeared on Claire's face. "Stanley's leash got tangled around my feet and I fell."

"Did you hurt yourself?"

"No. I'm okay."

"I should call your father. He'll be worried."

Claire's face crumpled. "I don't want to go home." Tears welled up in the girl's eyes. She wiped at them with her hand, smearing mud on her face. "He's going to take us far away. I heard him say so."

Anne quickly put her arms around Claire. "Oh, sweetie. It's going to be okay."

"No, it's not," she sobbed. "He's moving to Denver and I don't want to go. I want to stay here with you and Aunt Lily."

"Denver?" Anne straightened abruptly. "Are you sure?"

"He said that. To Manny. I heard him."

"I'm going to call your father, right now."

Claire shook her head, a fierce expression on her splotchy face. "I don't want to go to back to Denver. I love Paradise. Please, can I live with you?"

"Why don't I ask him if you can stay over? He can pick you up on Saturday. You and I can have a little vacation together. We'll figure out what's going on with Denver, too."

Claire's face lit up. "Yes, please."

"Okay, you go to the porch and take off your sneakers and roll up your pant legs. I'll be right there."

Claire smiled and nodded, running toward the back of the house.

Anne pulled out her cell and looked up Matt's number.

"Matt, it's Anne. Claire is here."

"Here where? At the hospital?"

"No. I'm at home. She's here and she's fine."

"How is it I can manage a crew of grown men

but I can't keep an eye on a little girl? This is the second time she's gotten lost."

"She's not lost. She's right here with me."

"You know what I mean. I was on my way over."

"No need. She's fine, except she's certain you're moving to Denver."

Matt groaned. "I knew she overheard me talking to Manny."

"Are you?"

"Am I what?"

"Moving to Denver."

"I don't know. At this point, it's only under discussion."

"That's too bad." She released a breath before the words spilled out. "Because I don't want you and Claire to leave Paradise."

There was silence on the line.

"I'm sorry, but it's true," she admitted.

"Don't be sorry," he said into the silence that once again had fallen between them.

"Well, obviously, I've left you speechless."

"I don't know what to say," he admitted.

"There's no need to say anything. I guess I didn't realize it myself until she told me you were moving."

"I'm not moving. Manny and I were talking. Like I said, it was just a discussion. I'm sorry I wasn't more discreet."

"Well, she's pretty upset. What about letting Claire spend the night here?"

"I don't want to impose. And I don't want to reward her for running away."

"It's not imposing when it's my idea…"

"And?" Matt urged her on.

"The first year after a loss is the hardest. I think you should consider cutting Claire a little slack. I don't think this can be considered a pattern of behavior."

"No?"

"No. Besides, I took off this afternoon and tomorrow. I'd love to have her. Aunt Lily will love it, as well. You can pick her up on Saturday."

"Saturday? Are you sure?"

"Very. But I'll need to get her insulin and some clean clothes."

"She has a house key in her backpack," Matt said.

"Oh, and by the way, I've got Stanley, too."

"Dog food is in the pantry closet in the kitchen."

"You know this will be good practice for me."

"Being a mom for a few days?"

"I meant being a dog owner."

Matt merely chuckled.

Anne slipped the phone back into her purse. A mom? She doubted that. Being a dog mom was probably as close as she'd ever get.

* * *

Anne turned the key and stepped into Matt's house. The smell of burned popcorn lingered in the air. She tiptoed through the living room and then paused before she remembered that no one was home. The quiet was unnerving and it seemed totally wrong to be in his house when he wasn't there.

She walked past the living room where Stanley's throw toys were scattered on the floor, and straight to Claire's bedroom. Fifteen minutes earlier she'd left the little girl asleep on the couch where she had been watching a television game show with Aunt Lily. The two of them had been calling out answers at the screen and laughing before Claire had finally nodded off.

Claire had given her instructions on what to bring and Anne easily found the requested items in the well-organized drawers.

The stuffed animals were lined up on the bed. The patterned pink spread that covered the bed was taut with each side perfectly angled at the same distance from the floor. The pillows were fluffed, the edges touching each other in a straight line.

Anne chuckled. Not unlike her own room.

Everything in the room was neat and tidy. Like Claire. It hadn't escaped Anne how much alike she and the little girl were. Orderliness was sometimes to control a world that seemed, at best, out of control. She definitely understood that. Though Anne was coming to understand just how rigid and inflexible the life she had created for herself in the past ten years was.

Maybe it was time to begin to step out of the shadow of the old Anne and start to loosen up. She headed to the kitchen with a small stack of fresh clothes and a clean pair of sneakers. Inching aside diabetic literature and a Bible, she set the clothes on the table.

First she filled a plastic bag with dry food for Stanley, and then she turned to locate Claire's needed medication. The refrigerator was impressively well-stocked and Anne had to move containers to find the insulin pens. Two casserole dishes took up most of the space on the shelves.

The Paradise ladies auxiliary was still bringing over food? No doubt the women in town absolutely loved every minute of delivering the dishes to Matt.

One foil container held a note with a recent date and described the casserole as Minnie's pasta bake. Anne was familiar with Minnie St. Claire, an elderly widow in town. The other was covered with clear wrap and the note on top simply included a phone number with a heart drawn in red ink and the words "Call me."

Matt remained the heartthrob of the auxiliary, it seemed. For a moment jealousy tangled its roots in Anne's mind. She resisted the urge to copy the number down to find out who it belonged to. Then she discarded the thought. She didn't really want to know. And, besides, Matt wasn't a man who sought attention. That wasn't him at all and it never would be.

Anne grabbed the insulin and scooped up the clothes and plastic bag. When she turned, the Bible slid off the table and onto the floor. She sighed at her carelessness and placed everything that was in her arms on the counter to retrieve the good book. The pages had flipped open to the middle, exposing a faded color photograph with worn edges that served as a placeholder.

A small gasp slipped from her lips when she picked it up and realized exactly what she held in her hands.

Her and Matt on their wedding day. Anne had never seen this picture and she herself had no such mementos of that day. Just her own memories that she'd tucked away and only brought out to examine and savor in the late hours of the night.

A smile curved her lips at the sight of both of them in their Sunday best at the office of the justice of the peace. The dress she wore had long ago been discarded, but at that time it had been the most sophisticated outfit she'd owned. They were kids, and so much in love.

She caught her breath at what was evident in

both their eyes as they looked at each other. Matt had offered her his heart so freely that day. She'd been a different person then. Impulsive, hopeful and deeply in love.

She had wanted to wait for a church wedding, but he had suggested the justice of the peace and begged her to concede to his wishes for them to be joined together right away as husband and wife.

She had, and five hours later they were apart again.

All these years later she'd wondered why he hadn't fought her aunt's edict. Why he hadn't come for her.

Anne turned the photo over. On the back in Matt's distinctive handwriting was a scripture reference. Psalm 31:24. She pulled the Bible into her lap as she sank to the kitchen floor. Unsteady fingers flipped through the thin pages until she found Psalms and read the verse aloud.

"Be of good courage and he shall strengthen your heart, all ye that hope in the Lord."

For moments she stared at the page until her vision blurred and a drop of moisture plopped down onto the Bible's delicate parchment pages. She wiped it away with her finger and then wiped at her eyes with the back of her hand.

She still loved him.

She'd never stopped loving him.

Anne scrambled to her feet and put the photo

and the Bible back on the table. But how could he ever love a woman who was once persuaded to turn her back on their love? How could he love her back without doubting her feelings?

An impossible situation.

Chapter Twelve

Lily Gray sat in the yard, wearing a large floppy yellow sun hat. Her throne was a bright red Adirondack chair. Stanley lounged at her side, looking for the entire world as though he belonged there. He barely acknowledged Matt; instead, the Lab happily thumped his tail while his gaze never left the elderly woman.

"Morning, Ms. Gray."

"Matthew. What a nice surprise. I gave Stanley a few biscuits. He assured me that it would be all right with you."

Matt gave a silent chuckle. "Certainly. It looks like he's decided to stay, too."

"Dogs and small children like me. Adults are less easily persuaded."

He arched a brow at the random comment. "Ah, were you saving this seat for someone?"

"My aide was sitting here. She's in the house making us lemonade. So please sit down."

"Thank you."

"I thought you weren't supposed to be here until Saturday. It's Friday, correct?"

"Yes, ma'am." Matthew glanced around. "Is Claire okay?"

"Oh, yes. She was upset. But she's calmed down. Apparently she was under the impression that you were moving to Denver. I told her that was absolutely ridiculous. You wouldn't go. Especially now that you and Anne have found each other again."

Matt nearly choked.

"Ma'am?"

Lily pierced him with her gaze. "Sometimes it takes me a while to figure things out, but eventually I do."

Was Lily Gray's mental acuity as clear as it seemed today?

He nodded but said nothing, afraid of what might be about to unfold.

"I was wrong, young man, and I owe you an apology for what I did. Ten years late, I'm afraid. But there it is."

Matt was too stunned to respond.

Once again Lily stared deep into his eyes. "You're still in love with her."

"Yes." He nodded, unable to offer anything else but the truth.

She shook her head very slowly. "Ten years ago I did what I thought was best for Anne. I chose to overlook the fact that you were the best thing for her."

"I thought it was because I wasn't..."

"Good enough? Did I say that? If I did, then I apologize again. No doubt I could have come up with any number of reasons. I didn't want you to take Anne away from me. That was the bottom line. A very selfish decision on my part. All parties involved have paid the price for my choices. I can only hope you'll forgive me and her."

"Forgiveness is a decision. A step of faith. I've forgiven. The hard part is the pride."

"A wise man, as well, I see. We've all got a mountain of pride that stands between us and happiness."

"I've got a lot to learn, Ms. Gray."

"Don't we all?" She offered him an indulgent smile. "Anne is still in love with you, of course. Perhaps she hasn't always realized that, but she's had plenty of opportunities to marry. There have been suitors, but she turns them all away."

He held his breath, knowing that he lived in a world where the other shoe always dropped. Would it today?

"I think you and I should come up with a solution to our problem."

"What problem is that, ma'am?"

Lily waved a hand in the air and the voluminous sleeves of her white blouse waved in the breeze. "Oh, you know. The house, Anne, Claire and you."

His head jerked back. "You know about the house?"

"Of course. I'm old, not dead."

Matt coughed. "Yes. I mean no, ma'am."

"I've gotten several phone calls from my so-called old friends who are angry because Anne and I are the only holdouts." She frowned and her voice slowed as if she was trying to sort out the facts. "That is correct, isn't it? We are the only holdouts."

"Yes, ma'am."

"I see." She stared straight ahead through the woods, as if she could see the lake in her mind's eye.

"I'm sorry to say that my company planned the road that will be going through here."

"Progress. I used to be all about that, too, once. Made a living on it." Lily shrugged. "The town needs that road, I imagine."

"It does."

"Then progress will prevail. So the obvious thing to do is to find a way around the situation."

"A way around?"

"Of course. I know people in the valley, lots of people in the construction industry. Surely putting our heads together we can fix this."

"I don't know. I've put my head together with

a half dozen people lately and haven't come up with a viable option."

"But none of them were Lily Gray."

"True. What did you have in mind?"

"They want the land and we want the house. It seems obvious."

Matt blinked and then was very still as her words penetrated. *"You want to move the house?"*

"As I said, you're a very clever man."

"There are quite a lot of details that encompass moving a house."

"Such as?"

"The cost is pretty hefty, especially when you consider both the size and age of this particular house. Then we've got to find enough land to do justice to your Victorian."

"Don't forget the rose garden. That must come, as well. Some of those blooms are as old as this house."

"Ma'am, this is a huge undertaking you're talking about."

"Yes, but what's that saying? About attempting something large enough that failure is guaranteed without God's help?"

"That's pretty much how it goes."

"And theoretically if all your details were attended to, it is a possibility. Correct?"

"Details? Yes. That's right." He said the words slowly, afraid of what might be coming next.

Lily was lost in deep thought for moments.

Matt cleared his throat and she looked up. "Does your niece…I mean does Anne…?"

"Does she know that I am aware of the situation?"

Matt nodded.

"No, she's protecting me. Isn't that sweet? She's been protecting me for far too long. I'm not as frail as she thinks. My mind may be Swiss cheese some days, but the rest of me will hang in there for quite a few more years."

Matt didn't know what to say to that.

Lily met his gaze. "It's time to shake things up around here. Time for her to have a life of her own."

Once again Matt didn't know what to say so he remained silent, desperately trying to determine if Lily was lucid or leading him down a rabbit hole.

"Overdue, too. Don't you think?"

"Um…" He floundered for an answer.

She glanced at the antique silver watch on her thin wrist. "Goodness, look at the time, you'd better get going if you're going to stop her."

"Stop who?"

"Anne."

"I don't understand."

"Anne and Claire have gone into town for lunch at Patti Jo's. Then Anne is going to sign the contract to allow the town to take the house in thirty days."

He stood and scratched his head. "You want me to stop her?"

"Of course I do, and while you're gone I'll get the ball rolling."

"Rolling how?

"It's time for Lily Gray to call in a few favors." She waved a regal hand in the air. "I've got things under control, don't you worry. Sometimes it takes people a little bit of time to realize I mean business." Lily narrowed her eyes. "I always mean business."

"Yes, ma'am. I believe you do."

"Good. So if you get a phone call or two from some of my contacts, you need to heed their instruction immediately."

"Okay. I can do that."

"All right, then. Go stop Anne. I'll let you know as soon as I have everything set."

Matt turned to go and then faced Lily Gray. "What were you going to do if I hadn't showed up here today like I did?"

"I always have a plan B. I called Sheriff Sam Lawson." She smiled. "I was going to have him find you. Oh, I think I hear his patrol car now. He'll take you to town expeditiously."

* * *

Anne instinctively eased up on the gas pedal when a patrol car passed them from the other direction with the lights on and the siren screeching.

She couldn't help but quickly glance over her shoulder in stunned surprise. "I think your father was in that patrol car with Sheriff Lawson."

"My father?" Claire, too, glanced behind her for a moment before looking at Anne.

"I think so." Anne looked in her rearview mirror. "Wait. They stopped. Are they turning around?"

Once again Claire twisted around in her seat. "Uh-huh. They are."

"I'd better pull over."

"Are we in trouble?"

"I doubt it, but this is Paradise. You never know."

Anne eased the truck off the road and unsnapped her seat belt.

"Stay in the car, Claire."

She strode toward the patrol car as Matt and Sam got out. "Is everything all right, Matt?" She looked at Sam. "My aunt is okay?"

"She's fine," Sam said. He tilted back his Stetson with one finger and grinned.

"Better than fine today," Matt agreed.

"I guess I can leave you here, Matt?" Sam asked.

"Yeah. Thanks, Sam."

"Good luck." The men shook hands and Sam headed to his patrol car.

"What's going on?" she asked.

"Anne, don't sign the paperwork yet."

"Why not?"

"Well, I can't actually tell you why not. You're going to have to trust me."

"I don't follow you, Matt."

"I've got a plan and I'm going to need a big leap of faith on your part. I'm asking you to give me a little more time before you go in to sign the paperwork." He offered a sheepish shrug. "But I can't tell you why."

"How much time?"

"I don't know yet."

Anne tipped her head back and looked at him. "Nothing can stop the inevitable. I have an appointment at the mayor's office at one to sign. Besides, what if your plan doesn't work? The town will simply file the paperwork and force us to move."

"That sort of thing isn't done overnight. It will require getting someone to serve you. That would be Sam, and since he assured me he'll be very busy when the paperwork comes through, as will Ed, his deputy, I am thinking you don't have to worry about that right away."

"But your business is going to be losing

money. You said so. I'd rather give up the house than hurt your livelihood."

A tender smile lingered on his lips. "What did you say?" he asked quietly.

"Matt, I know how much this project means for your company. You've come so far and I'm thrilled for you and Manny. I don't want to be responsible for its ruin."

"Thank you for saying that." He smiled into her eyes. "But you must realize that I feel the same way. I don't want to be responsible for you losing your home."

"So once again we're at a standoff?"

"No. Not if you can just trust me for a little while. There are other things going on that I can't share with you right now."

"Sure, I can do that." She paused and released a breath. "I owe you that much."

"No, I want you to do it because that's how far we've come, not because you owe me."

Anne met his intense gaze; her eyes following the firm set of his jaw, the resoluteness there. "I trust you, Matt."

He put a hand on her shoulder. "Thanks."

She nodded, warmed by the simple touch.

"I guess I need a ride," he said, glancing down the road.

"We were on our way to lunch. Would you like to join us?"

"Sure. But Claire might not want me along."

"I can find something to do, so you two can talk."

He shook his head. "The three of us have been through too much to have secrets now." Matt walked to the passenger door and tapped on the window.

Claire opened the door and Matt hovered in the door frame, his arm stretched across the roof of the small pickup.

"Mind if I join you and Anne for lunch?"

The little girl just sat there, twisting her hands in her lap with her eyes firmly fixed on her shoes.

"Can you look at me, please?"

Slowly, Claire raised her chin. Her lips quivered for a moment and then she met his gaze.

"We are not moving to Denver." He offered a reassuring smile along with the words he knew she needed to hear.

"We aren't?" Hope flickered in her eyes.

"No. I'm sorry you heard that. But you have to remember that what you were doing is called eavesdropping. And there is an old saying about that. Eavesdroppers seldom hear anything good."

"What's that mean?"

"It means that you should have come to me right away. The fact is, you didn't hear all of the conversation. If you had you would know I was only talking because I was frustrated."

"I'm sorry."

"So am I." He put a finger beneath her chin. "But running away is never the answer. I'm your father and you have to believe in your heart that I love you and I would never do anything that wasn't in the best interest of our family."

He paused. "Us. You and me. We're a family now, okay?"

She nodded. "Does that mean that we're staying in Paradise?"

"As long as Paradise will have us, we're staying."

His gaze met Anne's across the interior of the truck.

He saw the sigh and the silent rise and fall of her chest as she stared at him. Was he imaging it or was her heart in her eyes?

Family was what he'd said to his daughter.

From his lips to God's ears.

There was nothing he wanted more in this minute than for that to come true.

Chapter Thirteen

When the doorbell rang Matt hoped beyond odds that somehow it could be Anne and Claire. There was a time when being alone was plenty of company for him. Those days had disappeared when he'd moved to Paradise.

Everything had changed.

Instead of enjoying the quiet, he had paced the empty house for the past hour, missing them. Missing Stanley, as well.

He was ready to admit that he even missed Lily Gray.

Manny had declined his invitation to go to dinner so he could spend the evening with Delia and the baby. Manny was one fortunate guy. Even Sam Lawson had plans that included going to bed early so he could go fishing in the morning.

It was only five in the evening and he had

hours in front of him with nothing to do but watch the clock tick.

When he opened the door he found not Anne and Claire but two smiling elderly ladies in matching tan slacks and pink blouses. One held yet another casserole from the Paradise ladies' auxiliary in her hands.

"Mr. Clark?"

"Yes?"

"I'm Doris and this is my sister Dee. We're the Knight sisters. This is your final meal delivery from the auxiliary. Well, unless you'd like us to have the auxiliary extend your home visits?" They looked hopeful.

"Oh, no, ladies, you've done plenty already. I couldn't impose on your hospitality any further. Thank you."

He opened the screen and took the still warm container from them and placed it on the coffee table.

"Would you like us to come in and heat it up for you?" one of the women asked.

"No." He cleared his throat. "I mean, no, thank you. This is plenty."

"All right, then," a sister said. "We'll see you in church."

"Absolutely." He moved to close the door.

"Um, Mr. Clark?"

He turned back.

"Yeah?"

"My sister was wondering if you had met anyone in Paradise. We have a lovely grand-daughter…"

Matt froze. "Thank you for thinking of me, but I'm already spoken for."

Their eyes lit up with curiosity. "Anyone we know?"

"I can't tell you until I tell the lady in question. She doesn't know yet." He winked.

They sighed in unison. "How romantic."

As far as he was concerned it was the absolute truth. He was spoken for. By Anne. She'd realize it sooner or later, but sooner would be a lot better.

He lifted the foil cover. While it looked good, it had only been a few hours since he and Anne and Claire had shared a big lunch in Paradise.

What were Anne and Claire doing tonight, anyhow? Girl stuff, he imagined. He walked through the house again, restless. Maybe he could take Stanley for a walk. Except Stanley was with Anne, too. The traitor. The overgrown mutt loved Lily's house more than he liked his own home.

Matt grabbed his keys from the counter. He could take a walk by himself.

As he headed toward Main Street, his cell began to ring.

"Clark, here."

"Mr. Clark, this is Hollis Elliott."

"Mr. Elliott. What can I do for you, sir?" *And*

why is the bison baron of Paradise Valley calling me?

"Actually I'm calling because I want to do something for you, son."

"Sir?"

"I've got a nice piece of land that overlooks the valley that I'd like to give you."

Matt swallowed his stunned surprise.

"I'm very appreciative, sir, but I don't quite know how you came to decide to give me land."

"Lily Gray. I've owed her a large favor for a couple decades. It's time to pay that debt. She was clear in her suggestion that you might be in the market for some property and that a donation of land in your name would settle our score." He cleared his throat. "I like it when my debts are paid, son, so I hope you aren't going to argue with me on this."

Matt rubbed the bridge of his nose. "Sir, did she happen to mention what I was going to do with the land?"

"You're going to move a house there is what she said."

"Move a house there?" He shook his head. So Lily was moving forward, all right.

"That's all I know, except she seemed to think that she in turn owed this to you for something. Said this was her way of giving you a piece of Paradise, a future here in the valley, with roots for your family."

Matt could hardly speak past the lump in his throat. "Thank you, Mr. Hollister."

"No need to thank me. I'm simply the middleman. This is all Lily's doing. She's the one to thank. And while you're at it, let Lily know we're all square, will you? Once that woman starts pulling in her favors she doesn't rest until the job is done. I'd like to be able to sleep some tonight."

"I will. I certainly will."

"Give my secretary a call and we'll take a ride up to the property when you've got time."

"Yes, sir."

Lily Gray?

This was beyond his comprehension. He'd been wandering his entire life. Somehow the woman had managed to know what he'd needed before he did. The woman had not only provided him a lasting tomorrow in this valley but she'd given her official blessing to him and Anne.

"Now all I have to do is convince Anne that she and I have a future together in Paradise," he said aloud. Matt continued to stare at his phone. "And figure out how I'm going to help Lily move a one-hundred-year-old house."

"Can we sleep in here tonight?" Claire asked.

Anne and the girl stood in the turret room looking out at Paradise. The night sky was illuminated by a full moon and the mountains were visible in the distance. If the pine trees weren't so tall they could have seen the water on the lake by moonlight.

"We don't have beds in this room," Anne said. She glanced around. The room had been empty for years. The only piece of furniture was a rocking chair and a small wrought-iron table. On occasion Anne came up here to pray and to sip a cup of tea.

"Did you mean it when you said you'd never been to a slumber party?" Claire returned.

"That's right. Aunt Lily was a little strict when I was growing up."

"She was your mom?"

"Pretty much. After my mother died she was my whole family."

"Just like me and my dad." Claire chewed her lip, considering Anne's words. Then she looked up at her. "I can show you how to have a slumber party, if you want."

"Okay, but no sleeping on the floor. This princess needs a mattress," Anne said.

"Can't we bring one from the bedroom up here?"

Anne laughed. "I suppose we could do that. How about we bring the two twin mattresses from the guest room?"

"Why are you laughing?" Claire asked.

"Oh, I was just thinking about a friend of mine who says I'm not impulsive."

"What does that mean?"

"It means that she thinks that I would never drag a mattress up two flights of stairs at nine o'clock at night simply so I can fall asleep under the stars."

"But you are. So she's wrong."

"Yes. She is wrong." Anne smiled at the thought.

"Anne? Claire? Are you up here?"

"Aunt Lily?" Anne rushed to the doorway at the sound of her aunt's voice on the landing. "You walked up all those steps?"

Lily grinned as she slowly came into the room, leaning heavily on the doorjamb. "Oh, my." Her breathing was short pants of air. "I haven't been up here in years, and now I know why."

Anne pulled the single rocking chair in the empty room closer to her aunt. "Here. Sit down. You must be exhausted."

"Not at all. I took my time. Simply a bit winded." She eased into the chair and glanced out one of the tall windows. "It was worth it. I'd forgotten what a view there is up here."

"Whose room was this, Aunt Lily?" Claire asked.

"It was mine and my sister's. Anne's grandmother." A wistful smile curved her thin lips. "We were twins."

"Twins?"

"Yes. Identical twins. Her name was Rose. Lily Anne and Rose Anne."

"Like the flowers outside."

"That's right, Claire. I grow those roses to remember my dear sister."

Claire looked at Anne. "You were named after the twins."

"Yes. My name comes from their middle name."

"What happened to her?" Claire asked.

"Oh, the complications of delivery after Anne's mother was born," Lily answered.

Claire stroked the soft, paper-thin skin on Lily's hands. "I'm so sorry."

"You are such a caring child. Thank you."

Anne stared out at the night sky, suddenly realizing something about her aunt she'd never dared to consider. Lily Gray had lost everyone who'd meant something to her. It wasn't that she'd wanted to control Anne's life, it was that Anne had been the only person Lily'd had. She'd been trying to protect Anne because she hadn't been ready to lose another person she'd loved. Somehow that eased the sting of her disapproval of Matt ten years ago.

Anne leaned over and gently wrapped her arms around her aunt's thin shoulders. "I love you, this much, Aunt Lily."

"Why, dear, I love you, too." Lily reached out a hand to touch Anne's face. "Are you crying?"

"Am I? Maybe. But only because I love you so much."

"It's going to be all right, you know," her aunt whispered.

"Is it?" Anne knit her brows together, trying to follow the thread of the conversation.

"Yes. I've been praying and now I've got it all planned out."

Anne stood and looked at her aunt. "What have you got all planned out?" she asked very slowly.

"Oh, you'll see soon enough. Soon enough."

Anne offered her aunt a weak smile. She had no idea what Lily was talking about, but that was okay. This was a precious evening and she was glad they all were together. Tomorrow she could worry about the riddles of tonight.

"Go get those mattresses I heard you talking about," Lily said. "Then maybe you can make us all popcorn, Anne."

"Can I have popcorn?" Claire asked.

"Sure, we'll check your glucose first and see how you're doing."

"You'll be okay up here by yourself for a little while?" Claire asked Lily.

"Of course, I will. No need to worry about me. Go and get everything ready. And when I see you are all settled in your castle room, you can help me downstairs to bed. I'll sleep well, knowing that there are two princesses up here in the turret room tonight."

A tapping at the window roused Anne from sleep. Was it raining? She opened her eyes and nearly screamed. Matt stood on a ladder outside one of the turret room windows with his face smashed against the glass. His nose was sideways and his mouth was flat on the pane. When he realized that she saw him, he pulled away and laughed heartily at the expression on her face.

"Very funny," Anne mouthed as she patted down her bed head.

"I thought so," he said through the glass.

She put a finger to her lips and pointed to Claire asleep in a tangle of sheets and blankets on a mattress on the floor.

"What are you doing out there?" she mouthed again, trying not to wake Claire herself.

He held up a window-glazing tool and grinned.

Anne struggled with the window sash for a moment before finally remembering how the pulley worked. She opened the double sash enough to allow her to stick her head out and look at him and his position on the ladder. "Oh, my goodness, don't you have some sort of rope around you so you don't fall?"

Matt scoffed. "I'm a professional. I climb ladders all the time."

"Well, Mr. Professional, you've got the wrong window."

"I know. I already fixed the broken pane." He assessed the window she'd opened. "No screens?"

"Not in an authentic vintage Victorian." Anne glanced out at the morning view, her gaze moving past the top of the trees and straight to the mountains. She took a deep breath before she turned to Matt. "How could you fix the glass without coming in the house?"

"I did come in the house. Through the window. Then I climbed back out."

"Okay, but that doesn't explain what you're doing out there now."

"I figured I'd check the gutters while I was up here."

"Wait a minute. Let's back up a minute. I thought we postponed fixing the window."

"You postponed. I was bored. You have my daughter and my dog. I had to do something. Besides, I've given you plenty of time to sulk over that town meeting fiasco."

She straightened. "Excuse me?"

"We're moving on, Anne."

"Are we?" A smiled slipped from her lips.

"Yep. Besides, you're half asleep right now, when you wake up you'll be thrilled the window is fixed."

"I wasn't sleeping, either. I got up hours ago and showered."

"Sure looked like you were sleeping."

"I was merely resting my eyes."

Matt started to laugh, the gesture propelling him slightly backward. "Whoa. Whoa." He swayed again.

"Matt, be careful. That's not funny." Anne grabbed the front of his shirt with two hands and pulled him forward until he crashed against her.

"Oh" was all she could say as her head rested against his shoulder, and her heart thumped loud enough to echo in her ears.

"Thanks," he murmured as his lips grazed her forehead.

When his mouth moved on to caress the curve of her cheek, she shivered.

"That's the second time you've caught me before I fell. Think there's some significance there?" Matt asked softly.

She swallowed. "Yes. I prefer you in one piece."

"Just so long as you prefer me."

"I do," she murmured as she edged away from the dangerous warmth of his touch. He'd terrified her a moment ago and she was still shaking as much from that as from his touch.

"Why don't you stop scaring me and get down from that ladder. If you come to the front door, you can join us for breakfast."

"Oh, yeah. That's an offer I can't refuse." He paused. "Is your aunt up yet?"

"I'm sure she's been up for hours in her room having prayer time."

"Good. I want to chat with her."

"What about?"

"Oh, she and I have a project we're working on."

"You and my aunt? Are you kidding me?"

"Nope. Not kidding. She and I are in cahoots."

Anne laughed, but Matt only offered a secretive smile.

"I smell coffee, so she's probably down in the kitchen by now. Knock on the back door and you two can have a clandestine meeting while I wake Claire and help her test her glucose. Although, I can't guarantee the cone of silence or anything."

"We'll work around the lapse in security around here. I'll put this ladder away and go find her." He nodded. "Thanks for having Claire. I bet she loved sleeping up in this room."

"She did," Anne said with a smile. "And it was my first slumber party."

"Yeah. I remember you said that. You sure led a sheltered life."

"Not anymore." Anne nodded toward Claire. "Unfortunately, it took so much work to get the mattresses up here and then get Aunt Lily back downstairs, that poor Claire didn't have much time to appreciate her surroundings. Five minutes after we settled in to tell stories, she was asleep. She didn't even wake when I checked her blood sugar during the night."

A slow, knowing smile curved Matt's lips. "You'd make a good mom, Anne."

Anne shrugged. "I'm a nurse. Taking care of people is what I do."

"That's not what I meant. You'd make a good mother."

A warmth spread through her at his words, because somehow she knew that he was right. She would make a good mother. And maybe deep down inside the restlessness she'd been feeling was because she wanted more than a career ladder to climb.

"You're thinking awful hard, there, Nurse Matson," Matt said.

She blinked and shook off the thoughts. "Be careful getting down off that ladder."

"I will, but I have to admit it's nice to know someone cares besides Stanley."

Anne ignored him and began to close the window. "See you downstairs."

A smile was on her face all the way down the stairs to her own bedroom as she realized that she didn't mind seeing Matt's face first thing in the morning.

If only things were different, she mused. Right now all she had were regrets and that wasn't how she wanted to start her day.

Chapter Fourteen

Lily Gray stood in the doorway of the dining room, leaning on her walker, staring at the tidy stack of collapsed storage boxes. Displeasure was evident in the set of her mouth and her rigid stance as she glanced around the room.

Anne waited patiently, knowing that a storm was brewing.

"Where did you get those?" Lily asked.

"The boxes?" Anne asked from her position on the floor where she sorted through the contents of a drawer.

"Yes."

"Mac at Paradise Hardware special ordered them for me."

"I don't understand what you're doing."

Anne smiled, trying to keep things light. "Spring cleaning."

"It's August."

"Then I'm either very late or very early." She grinned at her aunt.

"Oh, now you're being ridiculous. You're packing, aren't you? Why?"

Anne looked up at her aunt. How much should she tell her?

Eventually she'd have to know the truth.

"Aunt Lily, we haven't cleaned out some of these drawers in years. Don't you think it's a good idea to downsize, just a little?"

Lily didn't wait to answer. "Matt just left. If you wanted to 'downsize,' why didn't you ask him to help?"

"I don't need any help. I'm doing perfectly fine by myself." She stood and cut a piece of tape to seal the next box.

"By yourself. I taught you that, didn't I?" Lily clucked her tongue. "I've got some repenting to do. I can only hope it's not too late to fix things."

"Fix things? What things need to be fixed?"

"You, to start with."

"What's wrong with me?" Anne inclined her head, waiting to hear the answer. Her aunt was in unusually rare form today. She wasn't sure if this was a good thing or not.

"It's me who was wrong, Anne," Lily said. "I was very wrong. Why I didn't realize it before now shocks me." She took a deep breath. "I raised you to be independent, but dependence on

Him is what I should have taught you. Can you ever forgive me?"

"Aunt Lily, there's nothing to forgive."

"I don't know how. I certainly messed things up."

"What are you talking about? Are you feeling okay?"

"Yes. I am perfectly fine, and I'm talking about you and Matt."

"That was a long time ago."

"But he still loves you and I know you still love him."

"Forgive me, Aunt Lily, but if I really loved him, would I have let you persuade me to leave him? Leave what we had?"

"Is that what's keeping you from reaching out to him now that he's back in your life? You second-guessing the past?" Lily shook her head, growing more and more agitated. "I don't know the answer to that. The only thing I am sure of is that Matt has forgiven both of us, so why can't you forgive yourself?"

"I don't know. I'm just not there yet."

"It's time for all of us to move on," her aunt continued.

"Move on?"

"Yes." Lily swept her hand through the air. "There's no time to waste with the town trying to put a road right through my dining room."

As the tape slipped from her fingers, Anne whirled around. "You know about the road?"

"Of course. When were you going to tell me?"

"I'm sorry. I didn't want to worry you."

"Worry me. Is that what's at the bottom of all of this? I've gotten so feeble you feel you have to protect me?"

"No. I... I..." There was nothing she could say that wouldn't hurt her aunt because, yes, she was protecting her.

"What's your strategy?"

"My plan has been to turn it over to the Lord. I don't know what else to do."

"Humph. Looks to me like you've given up."

"No, I haven't given up. I'm being practical. I want to be prepared. Why fight the inevitable?"

"You're giving up." Lily sighed and slowly shook her head. "I'm so disappointed."

"Aunt Lily, we don't have a choice."

"Nonsense. That's what life is all about. Choices."

Anne's head jerked up. "What exactly does that mean?"

"It means I want you to stop what you're doing and listen to me for a minute." Her tone was definitely one-hundred-percent Lily Gray. As her aunt's condition had grown worse, Anne hadn't expected to ever hear it again.

"Yes, ma'am."

"I'm trying to tell you that even I recognize that I'm having more and more muddled moments."

"I know, Aunt Lily, and I'd hoped we could stay in this house…" Her voice trailed off as she fought back the tears. "I thought it might help if we could stay in familiar surroundings."

Lily left her walker and navigated to Anne using the furniture for balance. She put her arm around Anne's waist.

"Oh, my dear girl, this house isn't going to save me. It's time to let go of the past and make some decisions for the future."

"What are you trying to tell me?"

"I'm ready to move to the retirement village. I'd have access to round-the-clock care. My friends are there."

Anne's chest tightened and her eyes pricked. "If that's what you want."

"It isn't necessarily what I want, however I can see it's what I need to do."

"I don't understand. If you want to go to the retirement village, then why are you fighting me about the house? What would be the point of standing up against the entire town for a big old house like this when I'd end up living here all by myself?"

"Because it's our house and it's a magnificent piece of history." Lily reached into the pocket of her sweater and pulled out a letter. "This arrived in the mail today. I got historic landmark status tentative approval."

"What? How?" She reached for the letter.

"At my request the committee escalated your application."

Anne burst out laughing. "Of course, you did. I forgot you're Lily Gray."

Her aunt gave a satisfied smile.

"I hope you realize that when I applied the old-fashioned way two weeks ago, they told me three months until the committee meets. How did you even know I filed?"

"I heard you talking to your friend Manuel. So I called a few friends in high places."

"Why didn't you tell me what you were up to?"

"Because it's not going to fix anything, and it isn't going to stop the town. I pulled a dozen strings or more and, yes, they're going to approve the house, but it still won't be final until after the deadline. Even I can only move the red tape of government paperwork so fast."

"I'm still pretty impressed."

"No need to be…yet."

"Excuse me?"

"Oh, yes, the best is yet to come, Anne. You just have to trust me."

Trust her. Isn't that what Matt had said? And Manny, too, for that matter?

Everything seemed to be a matter of trust lately.

Anne rubbed the back of her neck. She didn't

know if she should be worried or excited. At the end of the day she was right back where she started. With a deadline and a dozen decisions looming over her head, right next to a sky-high stack of maybes.

By the time Lily had gone to take a nap, Anne had packed half a dozen boxes and filled another half a dozen with items to donate to charity. She also had a pile of items to ask her aunt about. Who had the sterling-silver baby rattle belonged to? And the staid black-and-white photo of a young couple behind the foggy glass in the picture frame had to be someone in the family tree. But who?

When the doorbell rang she unfolded herself from the floor and moved to answer it before her aunt heard it and woke up.

Anne glanced at her watch. "Matt, what are you doing back here?"

"Not glad to see me?"

She glanced away from his scrutiny. His words couldn't be further from the truth. Every time she saw him it was a little bit more like coming home.

"Always glad to see a friend," she said. "I simply meant that you only left a few hours ago."

"Your aunt called me."

"Lily said she was going upstairs to take a nap."

"I'm sure she did, after she called me."

Anne held the open door for him. "Why did she call you?"

He chuckled. "She's your aunt. You'll have to ask her what she's up to."

"So you're telling me that you came all the way over here because my aunt told you to and you don't know why. That makes no sense."

He laughed again. "It will shortly. I promise."

Matt followed her to the dining room and assessed the disarray. "What are you doing?"

"Everyone keeps asking me that. I thought it would be obvious." She held up the tape and pointed to the boxes. "I'm packing."

"Okay, packing is good, except that according to the movers you only need to pack your valuables. Everything else can stay right where it is."

"What movers were you talking to?"

He frowned. "I, uh, I was doing research online…"

"You're doing moving research for me?"

He shrugged.

"What movers only say to pack your valuables? That doesn't make any sense, either."

Matt opened his mouth and then closed it.

"Are you sure Lily didn't ask you over to make me stop packing?"

"Your aunt was pretty agitated when she

called. She said it was time for me to show you something."

She cocked her head. "And what could that be?"

Matt took the tape from her and put it on the table. "Yeah. Have you got time to take a little ride?"

"Sure. Lily is taking a nap, so I have about an hour."

He took her hand and urged her toward the front door. Anne tried to pretend that the gesture meant nothing. Matt taking her hand the way he used to. But it meant everything and, inside, her heart soared.

"Where's Claire?" she asked as he unlocked the passenger door of his truck. Anne got in and reached over to unlock his door for him.

"She's at Delia's. They're planning Manny's birthday dinner. Claire is making your chicken recipe. She's pretty excited."

"Oh, I'm glad." She paused. "How old will Manny be?"

"Don't ask. He's old. Really old."

"You were roommates. Aren't you the same age?"

"Manny has an old spirit."

"That's the funniest thing I ever heard. An old spirit, hmm?"

"I'm telling you, it's the truth. He doles out advice like you wouldn't believe. The annoying part is that ninety-nine percent of the time he's right."

Anne laughed again.

They left the outskirts of Paradise and continued to drive farther into the valley that surrounded the town. Soon grazing bison could be seen along the rolling hillside.

"How far out are we?"

"Only about four miles."

"I guess I just don't remember this side of the hill. Isn't this part of Elliott Ranch?"

"The ranch spreads from here to over the next two hills and then some."

Matt parked the truck on the top of the crest and got out. Then he came around and helped her out.

"It's beautiful," Anne said. "The wildflowers are still blooming…and look at the mountains. I love this time of year."

"There's more. Listen," Matt said.

They stood together quietly with the music of nature around them, until Anne gradually tuned in to the sound of gurgling water.

"Is that a creek?"

He grinned. "Good ear. That's Whistling Creek. Wouldn't it be nice to fall asleep to the sound of that at night?"

"That would cure my insomnia," she agreed.

"You're having trouble sleeping?" Matt asked.

Anne lifted a shoulder. "A lot on my mind."

She turned around and took in the sight that surrounded her. "Any particular reason why you brought me to Elliott land?"

"This spot, right here, isn't his land. At least, not any longer."

"Whose land is it?"

"It's Matthew Clark land."

Anne gasped and turned back to him "What?"

"Hollis Elliott gave it to me."

"Gave it to you? Hollis Elliott doesn't just give away his land. I didn't even realize you knew him." She shook her head. "Why would he give you his land?" Her eyes widened and she stared, stunned, waiting for an explanation.

"Everything comes full circle back to your aunt. Mr. Elliott owed her a favor and Lily called it in."

"Matt, this is getting more and more confusing. What kind of debt could Hollis Elliott possibly owe my aunt?"

"Who knows? This is your Lily Gray we're talking about." His eyes sparkled as he spoke. "I don't understand what's going on, either, but I'm going with it, because I know that God works through people. Apparently right now he's working through your aunt and at least a dozen people she knows."

"A dozen people?" Anne shook her head. "You know, a part of me insists on knowing what's going on, and another part of me thinks maybe I don't want to find out."

"Oh, it's definitely time for you to know." He smiled. "It's pretty simple, too. That plan I was talking about? It's really your aunt who came up with it."

Anne cocked her head in question.

"We're going to move the house."

Hollis Elliott gifting the land to Matt had stunned her. This news had her mouth dropping open.

"Move the house!"

"I'd like to say it was my idea, however your aunt sort of led me down the path to enlightenment on this one." He chuckled. "Actually, we're talking about moving the house, the gazebo and the roses."

"We can't afford to move a house. That will cost a fortune. A fortune I don't have."

"I told you, your aunt is pulling in a lifetime of favors. She will move that house, so you may as well get used to the idea."

"We don't have enough time even if we wanted to."

"Sure we do. The town's lawyer is going to draw up an amended contract that will allow the town to buy the land and not the house. That will take some time. Enough for us to get a foundation poured on the property and then, literally, move everything."

"And who's going to handle the foundation?" she asked, already knowing the answer.

"I know a contractor who will do it for free. Your aunt has her contacts locating someone who will take care of the move for what the town is going to pay you for the land."

"Oh, my goodness." Anne put her hands to her face, almost giddy with excitement. "This might actually happen."

"Believe it, Anne. It is going to happen."

"So that's why we only need to pack the valuables?"

Matt nodded. "I talked to the house movers Lily contacted. According to them there's no risk of jarring, but they advise homeowners to remove valuables. Once a house is off its foundation there is an opening underneath in which anyone can enter. This may be Paradise, but we have a lot of seasonal traffic this time of year."

"I'm stunned. I never would have thought this was possible."

"Your aunt did."

She mulled that thought for a moment, her mind still reeling. "Why do you suppose she's been so mentally clear these past few weeks?"

"You're the nurse, you tell me."

"My guess is that working on this problem is actually good for her. It's been fun to see the old Lily back in action, wheeling and dealing," Anne said.

She turned around and really allowed herself to take in the beauty of the land around her. Then it hit her.

"Matt, this is your land. My house is going on your land."

"I'm hoping it will be our land."

Though he'd said the words clearly, Anne still couldn't comprehend the reality she was hearing.

"Anne, I've made some mistakes. Clearly, I didn't honor our love after you left. I was devastated and I'm not proud of the choices I made. But the Lord turned me around and gave me Claire despite the fact that I walked away from Him for a short time."

He met her gaze.

"That doesn't mean I stopped loving you. I've never stopped loving you. It took coming back to Paradise to make me realize that."

She stood very still, taking in his words. "But will you ever really trust me again?"

"Stop persecuting yourself for decisions you made at eighteen. You were right. I can see that now. You owed Lily far more than you owed me back then. She was the only family you had. I would have liked to have grown up with someone like her on my side."

"Maybe I was too loyal to my aunt."

"You owe her that. You'd only known me a short time."

Anne was silent, afraid to voice the question

deep inside, though she knew it was time. And then it was as if he'd read her mind.

"I take responsibility for what happened, too. I should have come to Paradise to find you long ago."

"Why didn't you?" Anne asked.

"Fear. Pride. When you're hurting you find a way to turn it into anger, as well." He shook his head. "Eventually, I realized that the timing was all wrong for us. I was ashamed that I had rushed you into marriage."

"You didn't."

"Yes, I did. You wanted to wait for a traditional marriage. I pushed for the justice of the peace."

"That wouldn't have changed Lily's mind."

"Maybe not, but if she'd had some time to get used to the idea, things might be different. I was so afraid you'd disappear that I pushed things."

"I did disappear and I let you down," Anne said.

"No. I had some growing up to do. I had to get to the place where I realized I wasn't alone. God was always with me."

"It looks like we both made mistakes. The question is where do we go from here?" she asked.

"Where do you want to go?" he asked softly.

She took a deep breath, savoring the question,

praying he was ready for the answer that was on her heart. The answer she could no longer hide.

"I think we have more than we did ten years ago. Now we have strong faith and a friendship, as well."

"That is, if you love me."

"Matt." The word was a whispered vow. "I've always loved you."

She was caught off guard when he pulled her into his arms.

A sigh was all she had time to utter as his lips met hers.

"Anne," he murmured against her mouth. "You have my heart. And my daughter's. I trust you with both."

She sighed again as she rested in the circle of his arms.

"So what about now?" he asked.

"Now?"

"Are you willing to take a chance on a future with me right now?"

"You always ask the hard questions," Anne said, unable to hide a smile.

"I have to. I'm not willing to wait another ten years for what I want."

"What do you want, Matt?"

"I want you in my life. Permanently and forever."

"What about Claire? What would she think about all this?"

"Let's see, she gets to stay in Paradise, she gets you for a mother. She gets Lily as her own aunt. She gets the turret room. What's not for Claire to love?"

Anne laughed. "Well, that's true."

They stood together looking out at the land for minutes, her hand in his.

"Ever notice how we never spend much time alone," Matt said, breaking the silence. "It's always Claire and Lily and Stanley or even Manny."

"Yes, that's because they're part of our lives."

"I know, but we haven't been alone since I changed your tire. Not really."

"What are you getting at?"

"I wasn't going to do this now. I wanted everything to be perfect this time."

"Perfect?" She turned to him, confused.

"I wanted to do the whole thing this time. Get all dressed up and go out to dinner and have violins."

"Violins? Do you even like violins?"

"No. You're missing the point here." Matt ran a hand through his hair and then frowned, his brows knit together in concentration. "Now, where was I? Oh, yeah. In a perfect scenario, I'd get down on one knee and ask you to marry me and the whole restaurant would cheer as you said yes and I slipped on your ring. But we're running out of time and who knows the next opportunity we'll have to be just the two of us."

Anne's ears perked. "Wait a minute. You bought me a ring?"

When Matt reached into the pocket of his jeans, she could only stare, afraid of what was coming. Afraid her heart would burst with joy.

"Yes. I bought a ring." A small jeweler's box lay in the palm of his hand.

"Remember the first one?" she asked.

"I'd rather not." He grimaced. "I think we got it at the drugstore near the college."

"I still have it. It's in my jewelry box."

"And I still have a photo of our wedding day."

"I know. I saw it in your Bible when I was in your house...

"So are you going to ask me to marry you?" she blurted, unable to wait any longer. "Because I think this is the perfect scenario." She gestured toward the majestic landscape behind him.

Matt grinned. "Yes, ma'am. I am."

She closed her eyes for a moment. "I can't believe this is real. I didn't dare to believe you could still love me."

His face became solemn. "But I do. Always. Forever."

Once again he leaned toward her and this time she eagerly reached for his kiss. Her heart pounded an urgent beat as their lips met.

Then Matt stepped away from her, suddenly distracted. "I think one of our phones is ringing."

"Hmm?"

"In the truck."

"Oh!" Anne stepped back, as well, still dazed from his kiss.

He strode to the truck and pulled open the door. "Yours," he said, holding her cell up.

Anne checked the phone. "I've had a message from Sam Lawson." She pressed the replay button and listened, then inhaled sharply.

"It's Lily. The sheriff's office received a notification from her alert necklace. She fell. They have her in ER.

"Oh, Matt. I hope she's okay."

Chapter Fifteen

Sam met them at the door of the Paradise Hospital emergency entrance. He nodded to Matt and fell into step beside Anne. "Seems a little odd, doesn't it? Me meeting you at the door instead of the other way around."

"It does. Very odd," Anne said. "What happened?"

He gave a short shrug. "Your aunt did everything right. She fell, used her necklace to call for help and didn't panic." He frowned. "I can't believe I'm going to say this, but it was a good thing that key was under the mat. That saved Jake MacLaughlin and the volunteer fire department from breaking down your door."

"How is she?"

"From the way she's been laughing with the staff for the past twenty minutes, I think your aunt is fine. Last time I stuck my head in she was asking about chocolate-chip cookies."

"Oh, thank you, Lord," she murmured.

"I'll be in the waiting area, if you need me," Matt said.

Sam's gaze followed Matt as he left, then he turned to her while they crossed the floor to the exam rooms. "Looks like things are going pretty good for you two."

"I, um…"

"Oh, come on. I'm your friend. Don't make me hear about you and Matt secondhand."

"Sorry." She offered a smile of apology. "You're right on both counts. Things are going very well."

"I'm glad. Matt's a solid guy. You can count on him. And you deserve to be happy."

"Yes. He is." She smiled. "Thank you, Sam. For taking care of Aunt Lily."

He gave her a pat on the back. "My pleasure. I love Lily. Everybody does." He nodded toward Exam Room 2. "She's in here. I'll be going. You let me know if you need anything."

Anne pulled the chart from the wall. She gently knocked on the door and stepped into the exam room.

Juanita was at the foot of the bed talking to her aunt, while Marta stood at the head, taking her aunt's blood pressure.

"Juanita? What are you doing here on a Sunday? And Marta?"

"We had some staffing issues," Marta said.

She removed the cuff and turned to Lily. "Blood pressure is fine."

"Of course it is," Lily said. "Juanita has had me laughing since I got here."

"Excuse, me? Hello. Why didn't you call me?"

Juanita turned, her eyes wide. "Are you kidding? You take off one day for the first time in who knows how long and we're going to call you back in? I think not. Marta and I got things covered."

"You shouldn't have to work on a Sunday after being here all week."

"Small price to pay to get you to stay home. We'll take some comp time. Don't worry."

Anne simply shook her head and moved to stand next to her aunt. "Aunt Lily, are you okay?"

"I fell." Lily shrugged. "It happens."

"Nelson says it doesn't look like she fractured anything," Marta said.

"No lacerations or signs of a concussion?"

"Anne, she's fine. Your aunt tells us she got tangled in the quilt and landed on the floor. The bed was too high for her to get up by herself. Nelson ordered an X-ray of course and that's the only holdup."

"This has been a big day for falls," Juanita said. "We only just cleared out the waiting room. Your aunt is next in line. I told her she had to take a ticket."

Lily laughed. "She also told me she was working on a line of hospital gowns with sequins. Oh, Anne, can't you just see me in a pink hospital gown that glitters?"

"Did you give her anything?" Anne murmured to Marta.

"Not a thing. She's just happy. Your aunt loves to be around people."

"You're sure that's all?"

"Of course I'm sure."

Anne glanced from her friends to her aunt. "Could I have a few minutes alone with my aunt?" she asked.

"Okay," said Juanita, "but we'll be right outside listening in."

"Speak for yourself," Marta said.

Anne put her arm around her aunt and gently rested her head on her shoulder. "Oh, Aunt Lily. I was so scared. What would I do if something happened to you?"

"Something is going to happen to me eventually, you know. Besides, the longer I'm on this earth the more I'm ready to go home to the Father."

"I'm not ready for that."

Lily patted Anne's head.

"Matt asked me to marry him."

"Oh, thank goodness. About time, too. That's the best news I've heard in years."

"Is it?"

"Of course. Let's get this wedding going. No

time to waste. I'm not getting any younger and this is Colorado."

Anne straightened. "What does Colorado have to do with anything?"

"First flakes, Anne. They are always in September. You know that. We have to get that house moved and you and Matt and Claire settled before the snow flies."

"Oh, my goodness. I hadn't even considered that."

"What about next weekend?" Lily asked.

"Next weekend?" She blinked. "You haven't even been discharged yet."

"I will be soon enough. Your friends can help. We'll have the pastor perform the ceremony in the rose garden."

"I'll need a dress."

"Susan down at the Paradise Boutique will take care of you."

"Two weeks might work."

"All right, but time's a'wastin'. At least call Patti Jo and get your cake ordered. Get one like you saw last week."

"First I have to wait until Matt asks me to marry him."

Lily's eyes popped open. "I thought you said he asked you."

"He started to and then we got the call you fell. I'll have to ask him if two weeks is okay."

Lily laughed. "He's a man. Two weeks is pretty much about perfect."

A knock on the door interrupted them. "Here's our techs ready to take her up to X-ray," Marta said.

"I should go with her."

"Anne, you know Victor and Aidan. They're wonderful orderlies. They'll treat your aunt like their own mother. She'll be more than fine."

"Yes. You're right. Let me know the minute the film is ready, will you?"

Anne strode across the department to the waiting area with a new determination. Matt was the only one in the room. He'd settled his big frame into an uncomfortable-looking, orange-vinyl chair and was staring at the floor as the big-screen television droned on in the background.

"Matt, I've changed my mind."

He stood, alarm on his face as he shoved his hands into his pockets. "Uh-oh. Look, Anne. Whatever the problem is, we can work around it. Is your aunt going to be okay?"

"Lily is fine." She licked her lips. "I…I want to get married. Now."

"Now?" His eyes rounded.

"What about the weekend after next?"

"I rushed you into a quick ceremony before. Are you sure you don't want a big wedding?"

"Yes. I've waited ten years for you. It's time. I

want to be free from the moat that I built around my life."

He laughed. "Spoken like a true princess."

"Do you think Claire would be a bridesmaid?"

"Does it involve a new dress?"

"Definitely."

"Then I'm sure she's in."

"Good. Now I've got to go find Juanita and Marta and ask them to be bridesmaids." She turned away.

Matt grabbed her arm. "Anne, wait. We were interrupted before. Let's do this right." Matt proceeded to get down on one knee in the middle of the waiting room. He pulled the ring box from his pocket.

From behind her Anne heard a collective gasp. She didn't dare look behind her.

"Marta, grab the remote and turn off that television," Juanita said. "We're about to witness history."

When he opened the box, a solitaire diamond ring winked at her.

"That diamond is huge," she murmured, her knees shaking.

"No, it isn't. It looks huge because the last one was so small. Now stop interrupting, I'm trying to propose."

She swallowed and nodded.

"Anne, I love you. I've loved you for ten years. Will you marry me?"

Her breath hitched so she could barely breathe.

"Say yes," Juanita whispered.

"Shh," Marta whispered back.

"Yes. Yes. I love you, Matt."

His shoulders relaxed as he took the ring from its bed of satin and slid it on her finger.

From behind her, the applause of the emergency room staff echoed into the waiting room.

She pressed her lips to Matt's in a chaste kiss.

Juanita let out a catcall and a loud whoop. "I knew this was coming. Didn't I tell you I smelled romance?"

Anne whirled around. "Ladies, we need to talk. In my office. Now."

"Uh-oh, it's never a good sign when the boss calls you into her office," Juanita said. "And right after she said I do, too."

"Is everything okay, Anne?" Marta asked as she and Juanita eased into the two chairs in front of the desk.

Anne smiled as she glanced down at the sparkly ring on her finger. She couldn't help but release a sigh. "I was proposed to by the man of my dreams in my very own emergency department. It doesn't get any better than that."

Marta frowned, obviously confused. "Then what is it?"

"I need your help."

Juanita shook her head and then gently tapped

her ear. She offered a short laugh. "Did you just say *you* need *our* help?"

"Very funny. Yes. I need your help."

"Whatever you want, you got it, boss."

"I'd like you two to be bridesmaids at my wedding."

"Ahhh! A bridesmaid. At my age. Yes. Yes. Yes. I am so in." Juanita jumped out of her chair and danced around the room before finally turning to Marta. "I told you matchy-matchy dresses were in our future."

"Wonderful," Marta said with a groan. "So when *is* the wedding, Anne?"

"In two weeks."

"Two weeks?"

"No worries, Marta." Juanita nodded confidently. "I have Susan's Boutique on speed dial."

"Lovely." She rolled her eyes and took a deep breath. "What will your wedding colors be, Anne?"

"I have no idea. Ladies, I'm turning all of the wedding preparation over to you two. That is, if you'll do it."

Juanita's shoulders shook as she silently laughed. "Of course, we will."

"I want it simple. You two know me better than anyone."

"We really get to plan your wedding?" Marta asked.

"I've got to sit down. I'm overwhelmed with joy and happiness. This is like a dream come true." Juanita fanned herself with a hand and then dabbed at the moisture in her eyes.

"Seriously, you're putting us in charge?" Marta asked with a concerned frown.

"You've asked me that twice. Yes. You have two weeks. How much damage can you do? We're getting married in the rose garden. The reception will be outside. We can rent a tent."

"Still, this seems highly unusual. All this spontaneity."

"I've had a reality check today, Marta. My aunt isn't going to be around forever and in a month my house is moving four miles down the road. We could get snow between now and then. So, if I'm going to do this, it better be now. I'm being spontaneous, isn't that enough for now?"

"That's the attitude," Juanita said. She leaned forward in her chair. "Would this be the time for some girl talk? Maybe, we can discuss that hunky man out there next."

Anne laughed. "No, we cannot."

"That's what I thought you'd say. And we did get to witness the proposal, so I guess I shouldn't complain. Too bad I didn't get it on my phone. I bet it would have gone viral."

"Juanita, no you wouldn't have," Anne said.

"Of course not, I know the rules. Still..."

* * *

Anne peeked through the French doors of the dining room out to the backyard where the celebration had already begun. Guests were filling the rows of chairs strategically placed next to the rose garden. A white tent filled the space beyond that and inside caterers were already setting up.

"We really pulled it off. In two weeks," Marta said. "We've got temp staffing in from Alamosa so everyone from the emergency room can be at your wedding."

"I see Megan is here," Anne said. "With Sam or with Luke Nelson?"

"Neither. She's playing her cards close to her chest. She finally figured out what I was doing and told me she'd find her own husband, thank you very much."

Juanita burst into the dining room. "I want to see the bride," she said.

Anne turned.

"Oh, my, my, my. You're going to make me cry. You look so beautiful. Where did you get that dress? I love that sweetheart neckline."

"Believe it or not it was my mother's."

Anne twirled around in the princess-length, oyster-white dress with the full petticoat skirt. She touched her hair to make sure that it was still in place. The sides had been pulled back and pinned to a headpiece of pink rosebuds from Lily's garden.

"You look amazing. The prettiest bride I can remember," Juanita sniffed.

"Both of you look lovely, as well."

"We do, don't we?" Marta added. "Even in matching dresses, though I can't believe I'm saying that."

"Anne, how does this look?"

Claire came in from the hallway in a pale pink version of the darker pink dresses that Juanita and Marta wore.

"Oh, Claire, look at you." Anne circled the little girl, taking in the tiny braids wound into her caramel-colored tresses. "Who fixed your hair like that?"

"I did," Juanita said.

"She looks so grown up," Marta said.

Claire whirled around, her arms spread wide. "I am grown up!"

"Did you test your blood sugar?" Anne asked. "We don't want to get too busy to check."

Claire nodded. "Not too high. Not too low…"

"But just right," Anne said.

"You two channel Goldilocks often?" Juanita said with a laugh.

"That's a family joke. Right, Claire?"

"Uh-huh."

"You're about to become a family and already you have inside jokes?" Marta said. "I like that."

"You are about to become Mrs. Matthew Clark," Juanita said. "A very impulsive, spontaneous and brave lady, and I am so proud of you."

Marta sighed. "So am I."

"Wait. Flowers. Where are the flowers?" Juanita said, looking around in a panic. "We need our bouquets."

"In the refrigerator," Marta reminded her.

"Anne, look," Claire called, excitement simmering in her voice as she stood at the French doors. "Aunt Lily is giving the signal. It must be time to start."

Anne turned and saw that Claire was right. Aunt Lily was waving her straw hat, the signal for them to begin their little processional down to the rose garden. She turned to Claire and took her hands. "I'm ready to be a family. Are you?"

Claire nodded and giggled.

Matt adjusted his tie. He turned to Manny. "You have the ring?"

"You asked me that two minutes ago."

"I did?"

"Yeah. Relax. This is supposed to be fun."

"I'll take your word for it." He cocked his head. "Do you hear music?"

"The Paradise band is set up in the tent. That's the wedding processional music. Look, up there."

He turned his attention to the house. Sure enough, the French doors had been thrown open wide. First, Claire stepped out onto the deck and slowly walked down the steps. His daughter. The happiness on her face was radiated in her big smile. She was followed by a grinning Juanita and then Marta.

Then he saw her.

The air whooshed from Matt's lungs and he nearly stumbled.

"You okay, man?" Manny asked as he grabbed Matt's arm.

"Yeah. I'm good."

Manny chuckled. "Yeah. You're good, all right. Best you've ever been."

Matt gave a distracted nod as he stared straight at Anne. Their eyes met and locked.

She looked like a princess in white. Suddenly he realized that he didn't have to apologize for staring, because the beautiful woman walking toward him was about to become his wife.

His wife again.

How had that happened? Given the circumstances, it was nothing short of amazing.

How had the Lord turned everything around and given him all the desires of his heart? Desires he hadn't known were there until he'd stepped into Paradise. He didn't understand, but he would never stop being grateful for God's grace.

Moments later and Anne was standing next to him, her arm tucked into his. Her gentle smile radiated the love in her heart and Matt was humbled.

"The marriage of Matthew and Anne brings us full circle, joining together two families, two unique stories with the one foundation of God. A new chapter in their lives is about to unfold."

"Amen to that," Lily chirped. The guests around her laughed.

"Who gives this woman to be married to this man?" their pastor asked.

Lily Gray stood slowly, leaned on her walker and offered a nod of consent. "I do. And about time, too." She grinned at both Matt and Anne before sitting again.

Anne turned to Matt. "God is so good," she whispered, her voice laced with awe.

"He is." Matt leaned his head closer to her ear. His voice was thick with emotion as he whispered, "I love you, Anne. With all my heart."

"I love you, too, Matt."

He glanced straight ahead. The green of the yard stretched for miles, meeting the silhouette of the mountains spread before them and creating a backdrop for this special day. The verse that the Lord had given him ten years ago when he'd first married Anne sprang from his heart.

Be of good courage and He shall strengthen your heart, all ye that hope in the Lord.

Epilogue

"Here it comes," Claire shouted. She jumped up and down with excitement right where she stood in the drive holding her father's camera, filming the inch-by-inch progress of the Victorian as it came closer and closer to its new home.

Anne clasped her hands to her chest as her gaze followed Claire's.

The huge semi lumbered down the road to the property Hollis Elliott had given to Matt, thanks to Lily.

A cheer went up from the citizens of Paradise who stood on either side of the road watching the truck's progress and waiting for the moment when the cookie-cutter trim of the house would become visible above the trees. Minutes later the turret room appeared as the house itself came into view.

Manny adjusted his sunglasses and yellow hard hat as he walked with purpose in front of the truck with a red flag in his hand. His gaze scanned the road periphery for any potential problems up ahead.

Behind the huge truck four more of the First Construction crew trailed the house, alert for anything that might signal a need to stop the progress of the move.

So far everything had gone without a glitch and Anne was grateful her husband's construction company and the Lord had partnered in this particularly special move.

"We have the land and now the house," Matt said.

"Our home," Anne breathed. "A historic landmark, thanks to Lily pulling some strings in Denver."

"She's got quite a reach, our Lily."

Anne nodded. "I can't wait until she sees the footage of this."

Matt laughed as he wrapped his arm around her. "That video is going to be interesting, with Claire jumping up and down like that."

"Lily will still love it because Claire filmed it for her."

"Are you sure you can't convince your aunt to live with us?" he asked.

"No. She's ready for the retirement community. She misses her friends. I also suspect she understands that her lucid days have become less and less. She doesn't want to be a burden."

"I miss her already and I can't believe I'm even saying that," Matt replied.

"No worries," Anne said. "She promised to come and visit and oversee the transplanting of the rose garden. However, you should know up-front that she made me promise to fill the house with children."

"Now that sounds like an edict straight from Lily Gray," Matt said. "No pressure, right?"

Anne laughed in response.

"Clear," Manny yelled to the driver as the truck approached the location where it would turn onto the lush green land that Hollis Elliot had sold them. The house would find its home on a new foundation looking over the beauty of Paradise Valley.

As Manny walked past Anne and Matt, who stood on the gravel drive behind Claire, he raised his thumbs. "God of the eleventh hour," he shouted.

"Amen," Anne returned.

Matt grinned and leaned down to kiss her. Their lips met and she realized once again how fortunate she was. This time there was no per-suading her to do anything but love her new family and their future in Paradise.

* * * * *

Dear Reader,

I hope you enjoyed the fourth book set in Paradise, Colorado. This story sat on the back burner for a while as I tried to understand the emotional and spiritual conflict of a couple separated by a well-meaning family member. A heroine caught between love and duty. A hero hindered by pride.

I found that I had to really dig deeper than usual to uncover the emotions of Anne and Matt. In the end the truth for both of them was that their hope and trust could only be in the Lord, and both of them had to learn to wait on Him. Our world is managed by a clock, but His world isn't. That's a difficult concept to grasp for all of us.

I hope this story resonated with you. Drop me a line to let me know. I can be reached at tina@tinaradcliffe.com or through my website, tinaradcliffe.com.

I'd really love to hear from you.

Tina Radcliffe

LARGER-PRINT BOOKS!

GET 2 FREE LARGER-PRINT NOVELS PLUS 2 FREE MYSTERY GIFTS

Love Inspired®

SUSPENSE
RIVETING INSPIRATIONAL ROMANCE

Larger-print novels are now available...

REQUEST YOUR FREE BOOKS!
2 FREE WHOLESOME ROMANCE NOVELS
IN LARGER PRINT
PLUS 2
FREE
MYSTERY GIFTS

٭٭٭٭٭٭٭٭٭٭٭٭٭٭٭٭٭٭٭٭٭٭٭٭٭

H E A R T W A R M I N G™
٭٭٭٭٭٭٭٭٭٭٭٭٭٭٭٭٭٭٭٭٭٭٭٭٭

Wholesome, tender romances

YES! Please send me 2 FREE Harlequin® Heartwarming Larger-Print novels and my 2 FREE mystery gifts (gifts worth about $10). After receiving them, if I don't wish to receive any more books, I can return the shipping statement marked "cancel." If I don't cancel, I will receive 4 brand-new larger-print novels every month and be billed just $5.24 per book in the U.S. or $5.99 per book in Canada. That's a savings of at least 19% off the cover price. It's quite a bargain! Shipping and handling is just 50¢ per book in the U.S. and 75¢ per book in Canada.* I understand that accepting the 2 free books and gifts places me under no obligation to buy anything. I can always return a shipment and cancel at any time. Even if I never buy another book, the two free books and gifts are mine to keep forever.

161/361 IDN GHX2

Name _____ (PLEASE PRINT) _____

Address _____ Apt. # _____

City _____ State/Prov. _____ Zip/Postal Code _____

Signature (if under 18, a parent or guardian must sign) _____

Mail to the **Reader Service:**
IN U.S.A.: P.O. Box 1867, Buffalo, NY 14240-1867
IN CANADA: P.O. Box 609, Fort Erie, Ontario L2A 5X3

* Terms and prices subject to change without notice. Prices do not include applicable taxes. Sales tax applicable in N.Y. Canadian residents will be charged applicable taxes. Offer not valid in Quebec. This offer is limited to one order per household. Not valid for current subscribers to Harlequin Heartwarming larger-print books. All orders subject to credit approval. Credit or debit balances in a customer's account(s) may be offset by any other outstanding balance owed by or to the customer. Please allow 4 to 6 weeks for delivery. Offer available while quantities last.

Your Privacy—The Reader Service is committed to protecting your privacy. Our Privacy Policy is available online at www.ReaderService.com or upon request from the Reader Service.

We make a portion of our mailing list available to reputable third parties that offer products we believe may interest you. If you prefer that we not exchange your name with third parties, or if you wish to clarify or modify your communication preferences, please visit us at www.ReaderService.com/consumerschoice or write to us at Reader Service Preference Service, P.O. Box 9062, Buffalo, NY 14240-9062. Include your complete name and address.

HW15

YES! Please send me **The Montana Mavericks Collection** in Larger Print. This collection begins with 3 FREE books and 2 FREE gifts (gifts valued at approx. $20.00 retail) in the first shipment, along with the other first 4 books from the collection! If I do not cancel, I will receive 8 monthly shipments until I have the entire 51-book Montana Mavericks collection. I will receive 2 or 3 FREE books in each shipment and I will pay just $4.99 US/ $5.89 CDN for each of the other four books in each shipment, plus $2.99 for shipping and handling per shipment.*If I decide to keep the entire collection, I'll have paid for only 32 books, because 19 books are FREE! I understand that accepting the 3 free books and gifts places me under no obligation to buy anything. I can always return a shipment and cancel at any time. My free books and gifts are mine to keep no matter what I decide.

263 HCN 2404   463 HCN 2404

Name _____ (PLEASE PRINT) _____

Address _____ Apt. # _____

City _____ State/Prov. _____ Zip/Postal Code _____

Signature (if under 18, a parent or guardian must sign)

Mail to the **Reader Service:**

IN U.S.A.: P.O. Box 1867, Buffalo, NY 14240-1867
IN CANADA: P.O. Box 609, Fort Erie, Ontario L2A 5X3

* Terms and prices subject to change without notice. Prices do not include applicable taxes. Sales tax applicable in N.Y. Canadian residents will be charged applicable taxes. This offer is limited to one order per household. All orders subject to approval. Credit or debit balances in a customer's account(s) may be offset by any other outstanding balance owed by or to the customer. Please allow 4 to 6 weeks for delivery. Offer available while quantities last. Offer not available to Quebec residents.

READERSERVICE.COM

Manage your account online!

- Review your order history
- Manage your payments
- Update your address

We've designed the Reader Service website just for you.

Enjoy all the features!

- Discover new series available to you, and read excerpts from any series.
- Respond to mailings and special monthly offers.
- Connect with favorite authors at the blog.
- Browse the Bonus Bucks catalog and online-only exculsives.
- Share your feedback.

Visit us at:

ReaderService.com